Acting Edition

MW01074073

Anastasia:
The Musical

Book by
Terrence McNally

Music by
Stephen Flaherty

Lyrics by
Lynn Ahrens

Inspired by the Twentieth Century Fox Motion Pictures
By special arrangement with Buena Vista Theatrical

From the play by Marcelle Maurette
as adapted by Guy Bolton

CONCORD
THEATRICALS

No one shall make any changes in this title(s) for the purpose of production. No part of this book may be reproduced, stored in a retrieval system, scanned, uploaded, or transmitted in any form, by any means, now known or yet to be invented, including mechanical, electronic, digital, photocopying, recording, videotaping, or otherwise, without the prior written permission of the publisher. No one shall share this title(s), or any part of this title(s), through any social media or file hosting websites.

For all inquiries regarding motion picture, television, online/digital and other media rights, please contact Concord Theatricals Corp.

THIRD-PARTY MATERIALS USE NOTE

Licensees are solely responsible for obtaining formal written permission from copyright owners to use copyrighted third-party materials (e.g., incidental music not provided in connection with a performance license, artworks, logos) in the performance of this play and are strongly cautioned to do so. If no such permission is obtained by the licensee, then the licensee must use only original materials and materials that the licensee owns and controls. Licensees are solely responsible and liable for clearances of all third-party copyrighted materials, and shall indemnify the copyright owners of the play(s) and their licensing agent, Concord Theatricals Corp., against any costs, expenses, losses and liabilities arising from the use of such copyrighted third-party materials by licensees. For music, please contact the appropriate music licensing authority in your territory for the rights to any incidental music not provided in connection with a performance license.

IMPORTANT BILLING AND CREDIT REQUIREMENTS

If you have obtained performance rights to this title, please refer to your licensing agreement for important billing and credit requirements.

ANASTASIA was produced at the Broadhurst Theatre in New York, New York on April 24, 2017 by Stage Entertainment, Bill Taylor, Tom Kirdahy, Hunter Arnold, 50 Church Street Productions, The Shubert Organization (Philip J. Smith: Chairman; Robert E. Wankel: President), Elizabeth Dewberry & Ali Ahmet Kocabiyik, Carl Daikeler, Van Dean/ Stephanie Rosenberg, Warner/Chappell Music, 42nd.club/Phil Kenny, Judith Ann Abrams Productions, Broadway Asia/Umeda Arts Theater, Mark Lee & Ed Filipowski, Harriet Newman Leve, Peter May, David Mirvish, Sandi Moran, Seoul Broadcasting System, Sara Beth Zivitz, Michael Stotts, LD Entertainment/Sally Cade Holmes, Jay Alix & Una Jackman/BlumeGreenspan, Carolyn and Marc Seriff/Bruno Wang and Silva Theatrical Group/Adam Zell; produced in association with Hartford Stage Company.

The performance was directed by Darko Tresnjak, and choreographed by Peggy Hickey, with sets by Alexander Dodge, costumes by Linda Cho, lights by Donald Holder, sound by Peter Hylenski, video and projections by Aaron Rhyne, wig and hair by Charles G. LaPointe, and makeup by Joe Dulude, II. Music orchestrated by Doug Besterman, vocal arrangements by Stephen Flaherty, dance arrangements by David Chase, Musical Director, Thomas Murray. The production stage manager was Bonnie Panson. The cast was as follows:

ANYA . . . . Christy Altomare

DMITRY. . . . . Derek Klena

VLAD POPOV. . . . . .John Bolton

GLEB. . . . . Ramin Karimloo

COUNTESS LILY . . . . .Caroline O'Connor

THE DOWAGER EMPRESS . . . . Mary Beth Peil

MARIA ROMANOV / MARFA . . . . Sissy Bell

TSARINA ALEXANDRA. . . . . .Lauren Blackman

PRINCE SIEGFRIED IN *SWAN LAKE* . . . . Kyle Brown

TSAR NICHOLAS II / COUNT IPOLITOV. . . . . Constantine Germanacos

DOORMAN . . . . Wes Hart

GORLINSKY / COUNT LEOPOLD . . . . .Ken Krugman

TATIANA ROMANOV / DUNYA . . . . Shina Ann Morris

VON ROTHBART IN *SWAN LAKE*. . . . . James A. Pierce III

YOUNG ANASTASIA / PAULINA. . . . . Molly Rushing

LITTLE ANASTASIA / ALEXEI ROMANOV. . . . . .Nicole Scimeca

OLGA ROMANOV / ODETTE IN *SWAN LAKE*. . . . . Allison Walsh

ENSEMBLE. . . . . Zach Adkins, Sissy Bell, Lauren Blackman, Kyle Brown, Janet Dickinson, Constantine Germanacos, Wes Hart, Ken Krugman, Shina Ann Morris, James A. Pierce III, Molly Rushing, Johnny Stellard, Allison Walsh, Beverly Ward

SWINGS . . . . .Kathryn Boswell, Kristen Smith Davis, Ian Knauer, ...Dustin Layton

ANASTASIA was first produced by Hartford Stage Company, Stage Entertainment USA, and Tom Kirdahy Productions at Hartford Stage in Hartford, Connecticut on May 12, 2016. The performance was directed by Darko Tresnjak, and choreographed by Peggy Hickey, with sets by Alexander Dodge, costumes by Linda Cho, lights by Donald Holder, sound by Peter Hylenski, video and projections by Aaron Rhyne, and wig and hair by Charles G. LaPointe. Music orchestrated by Doug Besterman, vocal arrangements by Stephen Flaherty, dance arrangements by David Chase, music direction by Thomas Murray, dramaturgy by Elizabeth Williamson, fight choreography by Jeff Barry, and voice and text coaching by Claudia Hill-Sparks. The production stage manager was Bonnie Panson. The cast (in alphabetical order) was as follows:

ANYA . . . . Christy Altomare

TSARINA ALEXANDRA / ISADORA DUNCAN. . . . . .Lauren Blackman

VLAD POPOV. . . . . .John Bolton

SUITOR / HOTEL MANAGER . . . . James Brown III

SUITOR / PRINCE SIEGFRIED IN *SWAN LAKE*. . . . . Max Clayton

COMRADE / COCO CHANEL. . . . . .Janet Dickinson

GLEB. . . . . .Manoel Felciano

TSAR NICHOLAS II / COUNT IPOLITOV. . . . . Constantine Germanacos

COMRADE / GERTRUDE STEIN . . . . Rayanne Gonzales

DMITRY. . . . . Derek Klena

GORLINSKY / PABLO PICASSO . . . . .Ken Krugman

COMRADE / ERNEST HEMINGWAY / COUNT LEOPOLD. . . . . .Kevin Ligon

MARIA ROMANOV / MARFA / ODETTE IN *SWAN LAKE*. . . . . . .Alida Michal

TATIANA ROMANOV / TATYANA / JOSEPHINE BAKER . Shina Ann Morris

COMRADE / RUSSIAN DOORMAN. Kevin Munhall

COUNTESS LILY MALEVSKY-MALEVITCH . . . . .Caroline O'Connor

THE DOWAGER EMPRESS . . . . Mary Beth Peil

ANASTASIA, AGE 17 / ANNA. . . . . Molly Rushing

ANASTASIA, AGE 6 / PRINCE ALEXEI ROMANOV . . . . .Nicole Scimeca

VON ROTHBART IN *SWAN LAKE* / DJANGO REINHARDT . Johnny Stellard

OLGA ROMANOV / COMRADE / CYGNET IN *SWAN LAKE*. . . . .
. . . . Samantha Sturm

SWINGS . . . . .Maxwell Carmel, Katherine Mclellan

UNDERYSTUDY FOR NICOLE SCIMECA . . . . .Riley Briggs

SONG LIST

Act I

CHARACTERS

In Order of Appearance

LITTLE ANASTASIA
THE DOWAGER EMPRESS
THE TSARINA
THE TSAR
GLEB
DMITRY
FIRST WOMAN
SECOND WOMAN
FIRST MAN
SECOND MAN
VLAD
ANYA
BLACK MARKETEER #1
BLACK MARKETEER #2
BLACK MARKETEER #3
MARFA
PAULINA
DUNYA
DRUNK #1
DRUNK #2
DRUNK #3
COUNT IPOLITOV
SMOKER
POLICEMAN #1
POLICEMAN #2
GORLINSKY
LILY
COUNT LEOPOLD
SERGEI
COUNT GREGORY
COUNTESS GREGORY

SETTING

Saint Petersburg and Paris

TIME

1906, 1917, and 1927

HISTORY

ANASTASIA was commissioned by Dmitry Bogachev and received support from the National Endowment for the Arts ArtWorks program.

A NOTE FROM THE AUTHORS

As one young woman told us after seeing *Anastasia* in early previews, "I grew up on the animated movie but the musical has grown up for me." And it's true. Like our title character, *Anastasia* has had a long and thrilling journey, from animated movie to the Broadway stage to international and touring success. Together, we three authors strove to make the story emotional and exciting – a romantic adventure rooted in history but inspired by a world-famous legend. And we've had the great pleasure of traveling the world together to see it performed, and watching audiences fall in love again and again with this story of a girl in search of home, love, and family.

Anastasia continues to resonate for us in new ways. On March 24, 2020, our beloved collaborator Terrence McNally passed away. But we know he would be absolutely thrilled that the show will be on another leg of its journey – to theaters, schools, and organizations all over the country and beyond. He would have loved to have seen your productions – done in your own way and using the power of your imaginations. And he would be overjoyed to know that like our heroine, theater is intrepid – alive and well and playing on – no matter what the world may bring.

So from our hearts, and on behalf of our dear Terrence, we wish you a wonderful production! "One step at a time, one hope, then another, who knows where this road may go!"

Sincerely,
Lynn Ahrens and Stephen Flaherty

ACT I

Prologue. 1906
A Small Bedroom in a Royal Palace

[MUSIC NO. 01 "OPENING FANFARE AND OPENING SCENE"]

(Icons lit by candlelight are the only source of light. There is a sense of suffocating luxury.)

(A little girl is being put to bed by her grandmother. The little girl is **THE GRAND DUCHESS ANASTASIA**, *the youngest daughter of* **TSAR NICHOLAS II**, *the Emperor of All Russia. The old woman, her paternal grandmother, is* **THE DOWAGER EMPRESS MARIA FYODOROVNA**.*)*

RUSSIAN CHORUS.
AH AH AH AH
HMM

ANASTASIA. Why must you go, Nana?

THE DOWAGER EMPRESS. It's time to go. I've stayed too long here.

ANASTASIA. Take me to Paris with you.

THE DOWAGER EMPRESS. You'll visit me with your sisters and little brother. There's a bridge there named for your grandfather, did you know that? *Le Pont Alexandre.* He never saw it. We'll walk on it together – and we'll go to the ballet every night.

ANASTASIA. Take me with you now.

THE DOWAGER EMPRESS. I already have, my darling

Anastasia. Wherever I go, you'll always be with me. You're my favorite. Strong, not afraid of anything.

ANASTASIA. Like you.

THE DOWAGER EMPRESS. Ssshh, our little secret!

> (*She gives* **ANASTASIA** *a small music box and shows her how to open and wind it.*)

[MUSIC NO. 02 "PROLOGUE: ONCE UPON A DECEMBER"]

Our lullaby. When you play it, think of an old woman who loves you very, very much.

FAR AWAY,
LONG AGO,
GLOWING DIM AS AN EMBER,
THINGS MY HEART USED TO KNOW,
THINGS IT YEARNS TO REMEMBER...

THE DOWAGER EMPRESS & ANASTASIA.

AND A SONG SOMEONE SINGS
ONCE UPON A DECEMBER.

> (**THE TSARINA ALEXANDRA FYODOROVNA** *enters on her way to a costume ball. She is superbly dressed in the style of the old Russia at the time of Peter the Great. She bows slightly to* **THE DOWAGER EMPRESS**.)

THE TSARINA. Have you said your prayers, my precious Anastasia?

ANASTASIA. Yes, Mama.

THE TSARINA. For your father, the Tsar; for your sisters and brother; for Russia herself.

ANASTASIA. Yes, Mama.

THE TSARINA. What's this?

THE DOWAGER EMPRESS. A music box. So the child will remember me.

THE TSARINA. Better prayers than music boxes in these difficult times.

> (*And now the* **TSAR NICHOLAS II** *enters. He, too,*

is dressed in full old Russia regalia and cuts quite a figure in it. **THE DOWAGER EMPRESS** *extends her hand. He kisses it.)*

THE TSAR. *(One last appeal to her.)* It's the last ball of the winter season, Mama. All Petersburg will be there.

THE DOWAGER EMPRESS. We've been through this.

THE TSARINA. She's right, Nicky.

(She cannot wait to be rid of this woman.)

THE DOWAGER EMPRESS. Remember, Anastasia: Paris.

*(***THE DOWAGER EMPRESS*** *goes.)*

ANASTASIA. Nana! Nana!

*(***NICHOLAS*** *knows how to comfort his youngest daughter. She adores him.)*

THE TSAR. The Tsar requests the first dance of the evening, *Mademoiselle...?*

ANASTASIA. I am the Grand Duchess Anastasia Nikolaevna Romanov.

*(The ***TSAR*** *bows slightly, then holds his arms out to* **ANASTASIA.** *They dance together in the old style. The music is very Russian. There is nothing "European" about the choreography. The ***TSAR*** *loves "being" Russian. So does his youngest daughter.)*

[MUSIC NO. 03 "THE LAST DANCE OF THE ROMANOVS"]

(Transition: musical and dramatic.)

(A brilliantly-lit ballroom in the imperial palace. The **TSAR** *lifts his little daughter, and the ballroom is suddenly crowded with elegantly dressed men and women, dancing in the latest "European" style. It is 1917. The music is completely different. Everything is the same, yes, but everything has changed as well. We feel the passage of ten years at once.)*

2 WOMEN & 2 MEN.

AH AH AH

(When the dancers part, we see ANASTASIA, now a beautiful young woman. She is the center of attention. It is her "name day." She is seventeen. Everyone wants to dance with her. She and her sisters dance together.)

2 WOMEN & 2 MEN.

DAH DYAHDA DAH!

DYAHDA DAH-DAH-DAH DYAH-DAH.

LYAH-DA DYAH-DAT DAH!

DYAH-DAT DAH!

DAH-DAH-DAH-DAH-DAH

(Now The TSAR, dressed in his finest military uniform, approaches ANASTASIA with the same open-armed gesture as before – in the nursery scene – and they begin to dance. They are a beautiful father and favorite daughter together. The absolute monarch of Imperial Russia and its radiant princess.)

(The TSARINA and the TSAR are presented formally, and all dance a grand, swirling waltz. Handsome uniformed cadets dance with the daughters. Note: All sing vocal accompaniment (AHs, etc.) which is specified in the score.)

CHORUS.

AH AH AH

2 WOMEN & 2 MEN.

DAH! DYAH-DA DAH!

DYAH-DA DAH-DAH-DAH DYAH-DAH.

LYAH-DA DYAH-DAT DAH!

DYAH-DAT DAH!

DAH-DAH-DAH-DAH-DAH

DAH! DYAH-DA DAH!

DYAH-DA DAH-DAH-DAH DAYH-DAH

LYAH-DA DYAH-DAT DAH!
DYAH-DAT DAH!

(Anastasia's **LITTLE BROTHER** *rushes forward in his sailor suit and cuts in. She adores him. She dances with him briefly. He does a little solo dance, but falls, and the* **TSARINA** *intervenes with concern.)*

(The family and guests gather together to have their photograph taken. On the first flash, the family poses alone. On the second, the family and cadets pose. On the third flash, the servants have joined the picture, too, but simultaneously we hear an explosion outside the palace.)

(All react as we hear shots, explosions, crowd sounds. The cadets go to the windows to see what's happening. More and more sounds from outside the palace. The guests are becoming increasingly anxious. There is a second explosion. The curtains billow and through them we see the red glare of fire.)

ALL.

AH
AH
AH! AH
AH AH AH AH AH
AH! AH! AH! AH!
AH AH
AH AH
AH AH

(The real world has infiltrated this elegant ball at the Romanov palace. There is a third huge explosion. The dancers and servants begin to flee. Some of the servants circle the Romanov family protectively, but they flee as well. Soon **ANASTASIA** *and her family are the only people left.)*

(The **TSAR** *and* **TSARINA***, their four* **DAUGHTERS** *and the* **TSAREVICH ALEXEI** *cling to one another and move as a group toward the door but* **ANASTASIA** *runs back to retrieve her beloved music box.)*

(As **ANASTASIA** *reaches towards it, there is an enormous explosion and flash of light. We should be stunned by them both.* **ANASTASIA** *vanishes into the explosion. The music box is gone as well. We have seen the last of the Romanovs.)*

(A light comes up on **THE DOWAGER EMPRESS** *in Paris, considerably older now. She is reading a telegram – for perhaps the hundredth time.)*

THE DOWAGER EMPRESS. All of them? All of them!

(She crosses herself in the Russian manner as the lights fade, and is comforted by her lady-in-waiting, **COUNTESS LILY***.)*

(Transition: musical and dramatic. We do not know what has happened to **ANASTASIA***. A new, more brutal kind of music is engulfing her world of ease and grace. Something has happened to the Old Russia, something terrible for* **ANASTASIA** *and her kind. Music builds…)*

Scene One
The Nevsky Prospekt in St. Petersburg
Post-Revolution Russia

[MUSIC NO. 04 "A RUMOR IN ST. PETERSBURG"]

(It is crowded, bustling with desperate people trying to eke out an existence. All traces of the Romanovs and Imperial Russia are gone. Instead, there are flags, political banners and likenesses of the Revolution's heroes. People are bartering for food, hawking whatever it is they have for sale or huddling around open fires to stay warm. Everyone looks undernourished and ill-dressed. The only ones actually working are some **STREETSWEEPERS,** *who move back and forth across the square with determined strokes. They are present throughout most of what follows, working steadily, sometimes as one, rhythmically, to do their job well.)*

(A young Soviet official is trying to raise the general spirits with what can only be described as modest success. His name is **GLEB VAGANOV.** *He is on his way up the new regime's ladder. His uniform suggests a low rank. He must shout to be heard over the grumbling discontent as he passes out pamphlets.)*

(At some point the projection that reads "St. Petersburg" in elegant Cyrillic changes to a blunt and bloody red before our eyes: "Leningrad.")

(Over the loudspeaker a chorus of Russian singers sing.)

CHORUS OF RUSSIAN SINGERS ON A LOUDSPEAKER.
(Pre-Recorded.) THE NEVA FLOWS
A NEW WIND BLOWS
AND SOON IT WILL BE SPRING...

GLEB. We hear you, comrades, the Revolution hears you. Yes, our way is long, the journey hard. The chains of the Romanovs were heavy – three long centuries they bound us – but we have broken them. Together we will forge a new Russia – a fair and compassionate Russia that will be the envy of all the world. That is the promise we have made, fellow Russian to fellow Russian. The Tsar's St. Petersburg is now the people's Leningrad.

> *(A young man has been listening with appreciable indifference. His name is **DMITRY**. He is poor and ill-fed but he has the kind of street smarts that don't allow people to feel sorry for him. He's a survivor, a prince among thieves. Right now, he's very restless.)*

DMITRY. They can call it Leningrad but it will always be Petersburg. New name, same empty stomachs.

THEY TELL US TIMES ARE BETTER.
WELL, I SAY THEY'RE NOT!
CAN'T COOK AN EMPTY PROMISE
IN AN EMPTY POT!

"A BRIGHTER DAY IS DAWNING.
IT'S ALMOST AT HAND!"
THE SKIES ARE GRAY, THE WALLS HAVE EARS

(To all, with ironic joy.) AND HE WHO ARGUES
DISAPPEARS!

DMITRY & ENSEMBLE.
HAIL OUR BRAVE NEW LAND!

ENSEMBLE.
ST. PETERSBURG IS BOOMING!
A CITY ON THE RISE!

FIRST WOMAN.
IT'S REALLY VERY FRIENDLY

SECOND WOMAN.
IF YOU DON'T MIND SPIES!

FIRST WOMAN. Shh!

FIRST MAN.
WE STAND BEHIND OUR LEADERS

SECOND MAN.
AND STAND IN LINE FOR BREAD!

ALL.
WE'RE GOOD AND LOYAL COMRADES
AND OUR FAV'RITE COLOR'S RED!

DMITRY.
NOW EV'RYONE IS EQUAL.
PROFESSORS PUSH THE BROOMS.

DMITRY & ENSEMBLE.
TWO DOZEN TOTAL STRANGERS
LIVE IN TWO SMALL ROOMS.
YOU HOLD A REVOLUTION
AND HERE'S THE PRICE YOU PAY!

ALL.
THANK GOODNESS FOR THE GOSSIP

MEN. *(Spoken in rhythm.)*
SPASIBO ZA SLUKHI!*

ALL.
THANK GOODNESS FOR THE GOSSIP
THAT GETS US THROUGH THE DAY!
HEY!
HAVE YOU HEARD?
THERE'S A RUMOR IN
ST. PETERSBURG!
HAVE YOU HEARD
WHAT THEY'RE SAYING ON THE STREET?!

SOLO MAN.
ALTHOUGH THE TSAR DID NOT SURVIVE,
ONE DAUGHTER MAY BE STILL ALIVE!

ALL.
THE PRINCESS ANASTASIA!

---

* Check online to hear Russian pronunciation.

SOLO MAN.
BUT PLEASE DO NOT REPEAT!

ALL.
IT'S A RUMOR,
A LEGEND,
A MYSTERY!
SOMETHING WHISPERED IN AN ALLEYWAY
OR THROUGH A CRACK!
IT'S A RUMOR
THAT'S PART OF OUR HISTORY!

SOLO WOMAN.
THEY SAY HER ROYAL GRANDMAMA
WILL PAY A ROYAL SUM

ALL.
TO SOMEONE WHO CAN BRING THE PRINCESS BACK!

(**VLAD POPOV** *enters.* **VLAD** *is a down-to-earth, good-natured semi-scoundrel who made a good living scamming the artistocrats, particularly the women. In their haste to depart Russia, they forgot to take him with them. It's been hard times for* **VLAD** *ever since. He's not really one of the new Russia any more than he was of the "old" Russia either.)*

VLAD.
They've closed another border. We should have gotten out of Russia while we could.

ST. PETERSBURG WAS LOVELY
WHEN ROYALTY WAS IN.

I CALLED MYSELF A COUNT
AS THOUGH I'D ALWAYS BEEN!
I HOBNOBBED WITH THE ROYALS
BUT THEN, A CHANGE OF LUCK –
THE TSAR WAS DEAD,
THE ROYALS FLED
AND COMRADE, NOW WE'RE STUCK!

DMITRY. Vlad, I've been thinking about the Princess Anastasia!

VLAD. Not you, too, Dmitry.

DMITRY.

> IT'S THE RUMOR,
> THE LEGEND,
> THE MYSTERY!
> IT'S THE PRINCESS ANASTASIA WHO WILL HELP US FLY!
> YOU AND I, FRIEND,
> WILL GO DOWN
> IN HISTORY!
> WE'LL FIND A GIRL TO PLAY THE PART
> AND TEACH HER WHAT TO SAY,
> DRESS HER UP AND TAKE HER TO PARIS!*

VLAD.

> IMAGINE THE REWARD
> HER DEAR OLD GRANDMAMA WOULD PAY!

DMITRY & VLAD. *(Sneakily.)*

> WHO ELSE COULD PULL IT OFF BUT YOU AND ME!

> *(**DMITRY** and **VLAD** rush off, already excited about their new adventure.)*

> *(A truck drives by and backfires very loudly. The sound would startle anyone but especially one of the **STREETSWEEPERS** who cries out and holds her hands in front of her face, palms outward, as if to protect herself.)*

ANYA. No!!

> *(**GLEB** has returned and now approaches the quivering young woman.)*

GLEB. It was a truck backfiring, comrade, that's all it was. Those days are over: neighbor against neighbor. There's nothing to be afraid of anymore. You're shaking. There's a tea shop just steps from here. Let me –

> *(He has put his arm around her. Reflexively, she stiffens and is about to push him away but she stops herself.)*

---

* Pronounced "Paree" here.

ANYA. Thank you.

> *(They separate.)*

GLEB. What's your hurry?

ANYA. I can't lose this job. They're not easy to come by.

> *(Her innate good manners briefly surface.)*

But thank you.

GLEB. *(After her.)* I'm here every day.

> *(But she is gone. **GLEB** looks after her, clearly smitten.)*

> *(Transition to the black market where **BLACK MARKETEERS** propose their various illegal wares to passersbys. No one is buying.)*

BLACK MARKETEER #1.

> A RUBLE FOR THIS PAINTING!
> IT'S ROMANOV, I SWEAR!

BLACK MARKETEER #2.

> COUNT YUSUPOV'S PAJAMAS!
> COMRADE, BUY THE PAIR!

BLACK MARKETEER #3.

> I FOUND THIS IN A PALACE
> INITIALED WITH AN "A" –
> IT COULD BE ANASTASIA'S!
> NOW WHAT WILL SOMEONE PAY?

> *(**DMITRY** and **VLAD** enter.)*

DMITRY. We need something of hers to show the old lady.

VLAD. There's more to being Anastasia than wearing a tiara, Dmitry.

DMITRY. Not much. Look how many people you fooled. *(To **BLACK MARKETEER #3**.)* How much is that music box?

BLACK MARKETEER #3. Ah, the music box! It's genuine Romanov. I could never part with it.

DMITRY. Two cans of beans, comrade?

BLACK MARKETEER #3. Done!

*(They shake on it. **DMITRY** returns to **VLAD** with the music box. Back to business.)*

DMITRY. Do you believe in fairytales, Vlad?

VLAD. Once upon a time I did.

DMITRY. We're going to create a fairytale the whole world will believe.

> NOW, IT'S RISKY,
> BUT NOT MORE THAN USUAL.
> WE'LL NEED PAPERS,
> WE'LL NEED TICKETS,
> WE'LL NEED NERVES OF STEEL!

VLAD.

> YES, IT'S RISKY –
> A LOT MORE THAN USUAL!

DMITRY.

> WE'LL TRY TO CROSS THE BORDER
> WITH OUR PRINCESS AND OUR PLOT!

VLAD.

> HOPEFULLY DISASTER WON'T ENSUE!

DMITRY.

> WITH LUCK IT ALL GOES SMOOTHLY

VLAD.

> AND WITH LUCK, WE WON'T BE SHOT!

DMITRY & VLAD.

> WHO ELSE COULD PULL IT OFF BUT ME AND YOU!

DMITRY.

> WE'LL BE RICH!

VLAD.

> WE'LL BE RICH!

DMITRY.

> WE'LL BE OUT!

VLAD.

> WE'LL BE OUT!

DMITRY & VLAD.

> AND ST. PETERSBURG WILL
> HAVE SOME MORE TO TALK ABOUT!

GROUP #1.	GROUP #2.
I HEARD IT FROM A PERSON	
	I HEARD IT FROM A PERSON
I HEARD IT FROM	
A PERSON WHO	A PERSON WHO
ASSURED ME IT WAS	ASSURED ME IT WAS
ABSOLUTELY TRUE!	ABSOLUTELY TRUE!

DMITRY, VLAD & ENSEMBLE.

SSH!

HAVE YOU HEARD?

THERE'S A RUMOR IN ST. PETERSBURG!

HAVE YOU HEARD

COMRADE, WHAT DO YOU SUPPOSE?

VLAD.

A FASCINATING MYSTERY!

DMITRY.

THE BIGGEST CON IN HISTORY!

DMITRY, VLAD & ENSEMBLE.

THE PRINCESS ANASTASIA,

ALIVE OR DEAD...

WHO KNOWS?

DMITRY & VLAD.

SSSH!

> *(People begin to hurry home, as dark approaches.)*

[MUSIC NO. 04A "UNDERSCORE AFTER A RUMOR IN ST. PETERSBURG"]

Scene Two
The Private Theatre of an Abandoned Palace

(It is dilapidated and run down. The Revolution has not been kind to it: there are broken chairs, a frayed theatre curtain, an out-of-tune piano. There is a remnant of a Romanov crest on the wall.)

(This is where DMITRY and VLAD have taken up quarters. They are not good housekeepers. The general squalor does not seem to bother them. Instead, they fit right in.)

(They are "auditioning" a woman for their "Anastasia." There are three candidates: DUNYA, MARFA, and PAULINA. DMITRY is running the audition. It's been a long, unsatisfying day. DMITRY's impatience and disappointment are palpable.)

MARFA. I am the Grand Duchess Anastasia Romanov.

DMITRY. Try it this time without the gum in your mouth.

MARFA. It's not gum, it's tobacco.
It's me, Grandmamma, your precious Anastasia. They shot me but I lived and I've come all the way to Paris to tell you I'm alive. I'm not really an actress.

VLAD. No!

DMITRY. Thank you, ladies, we'll let you know.

PAULINA. What you're doing is against the law.

DUNYA. For this we lost our best hours on the street.

MARFA. If you weren't so handsome, Dmitry, I'd report you.

DMITRY. Out! Out!

(The THREE WOMEN leave.)

VLAD. Well, you tried, my friend. Anastasias don't grow on trees.

DMITRY. I'm not giving up. I'll go to Siberia to find an Anastasia.

VLAD. Have you ever been to Siberia?

DMITRY. I've never been anywhere but here.

VLAD. The day I took up with you!

DMITRY. It was me or a Bolshevik firing squad.

VLAD. You saved my life.

DMITRY. A rash act of kindness. Completely out of character.

(*DMITRY is trying to open the music box.*)

VLAD. Stop fiddling with that before you break it.

DMITRY. I can't get it open.

VLAD. It's a fake.

DMITRY. How would you know?

VLAD. No one spots a fake like Count Vladimir Popov, the biggest fake of them all.

(*There is a knock.*)

DMITRY. I knew it, those women ratted on us!

VLAD. At least they'll feed us in jail.

(*ANYA enters.*)

ANYA. I'm looking for someone called Dmitry.

DMITRY. I'm Dmitry. What do you want?

ANYA. I need exit papers and I was told you're the only person who can help me.

DMITRY. Exit papers are expensive.

ANYA. I've saved a little money.

DMITRY. The right papers cost a lot.

ANYA. I'm a hard worker. You'll get your money.

DMITRY. What do you do?

ANYA. I'm a streetsweeper.

DMITRY. A streetsweeper!

ANYA. In Odessa, I washed dishes. Before that, I worked at the hospital in Perm.

DMITRY. They're a long way from here.

ANYA. I know. I walked it.

DMITRY. You walked here all the way from Perm?

ANYA. I had no choice.

DMITRY. Who are you running from?

ANYA. I'm running *to* someone. I don't know who they are but they're waiting for me in Paris.

DMITRY. You don't need papers. There's a canal out there. Jump in and start swimming. You'll be in Paris before you know it. *(To* **VLAD.***)* She's crazy.

ANYA. *(With real anger.)* I'm not crazy!

> *(Both men are taken aback by this flash of temperament.)*

Why are you so unkind?

VLAD. *(To the rescue.)* We were hoping you'd be someone else.

ANYA. Who?

VLAD. Someone who may not even exist.

> **(ANYA** *looks confused, dazed. She turns around as if to find her bearings.)*

ANYA. I've been in this room before. There was a play. Everyone was beautifully dressed.

VLAD. This was the private theatre in Count Yusupov's palace.

ANYA. People were polite and kind.

DMITRY. *(Annoyed.)* She's going to faint on us!

VLAD. When did you eat last?

ANYA. Afterwards, we danced. There was champagne. I stole a sip.

VLAD. Where are your manners, Dmitry? Get her some water – and a piece of that cheese.

DMITRY. This isn't a soup kitchen, Vlad.

> *(Nevertheless, he will get them and bring them to her.)*

ANYA. You seem to be a gentleman, even if your friend is not.

VLAD. Gentleman! I haven't heard that word in a long time. Life hasn't been easy for my young friend.

ANYA. Life has not been easy for anyone.

> *(**DMITRY** brings her water and something to eat.)*

Thank you.

> *(She drinks and greedily eats like an animal.)*

VLAD. *(To **DMITRY**.)* Don't be too quick about this one.

DMITRY. Her? Have you gone crazy, too?

> *(But from this point on, **DMITRY** will stare at **ANYA**.)*

VLAD. I'm Vlad. What's your name, dear?

[MUSIC NO. 05 "IN MY DREAMS"]

ANYA. I don't know.

VLAD. You don't know?

ANYA. They gave me a name at the hospital, Anya. They told me I had amnesia. There was nothing they could do about it.

VLAD. Tell us what you do remember.

ANYA.

THEY SAID I WAS FOUND
BY THE SIDE OF A ROAD.
THERE WERE TRACKS ALL AROUND,
IT HAD RECENTLY SNOWED.
IN THE DARKNESS AND COLD
WITH THE WIND IN THE TREES,
A GIRL WITH NO NAME
AND NO MEM'RIES BUT THESE:

RAIN AGAINST A WINDOW.
SHEETS UPON A BED.
TERRIFYING NURSES
WHISP'RING OVERHEAD.
"CALL THE CHILD ANYA."
"GIVE THE CHILD A HAT."
I DON'T KNOW A THING
BEFORE THAT...

TRAVELING THE BACK ROADS.
SLEEPING IN THE WOOD.
TAKING WHAT I NEEDED.
WORKING WHEN I COULD.
KEEPING UP MY COURAGE,
FOOLISH AS IT SEEMS,
AT NIGHT, ALL ALONE,
IN MY DREAMS...

IN MY DREAMS
SHADOWS CALL.
THERE'S A LIGHT AT THE END OF A HALL.
THEN MY DREAMS
FADE AWAY
BUT I KNOW IT ALL WILL COME BACK
ONE DAY.

> *(We begin to hear the ghostly voices of children, and see their vague silhouettes – something to foreshadow the dreams that are to come.)*

ANYA.	GHOSTLY VOICES (WOMEN OFFSTAGE).
	AH...
	AH...
I DREAM OF A CITY	AH...
BEYOND ALL COMPARE.	
IS IT PARIS?	
PARIS!	
A BEAUTIFUL RIVER,	AH...
A BRIDGE BY A SQUARE	
AND I HEAR A VOICE WHISPER	AH...
I'LL MEET YOU RIGHT THERE	AH...
IN PARIS.	AH AH...

> *(The voices / visions fade away.)*

PARIS...

(Coming out of vision, intimate, urgent, growing stronger.)

ANYA.

YOU DON'T KNOW WHAT IT'S LIKE
NOT TO KNOW WHO YOU ARE!
TO HAVE LIVED IN THE SHADOWS,
AND TRAVELED THIS FAR.
I'VE SEEN FLASHES OF FIRE,
HEARD THE ECHO OF SCREAMS.
BUT I STILL HAVE THIS FAITH
IN THE TRUTH OF MY DREAMS...

IN MY DREAMS
IT'S ALL REAL
AND MY HEART HAS SO MUCH TO REVEAL.
AND MY DREAMS
SEEM TO SAY...
DON'T BE AFRAID TO GO ON
DON'T GIVE UP HOPE, COME WHAT MAY.
I KNOW IT ALL WILL COME BACK ONE DAY!

[MUSIC NO. 05A "UNDERSCORE AFTER IN MY DREAMS"]

DMITRY. Maybe we can help you after all, Anya. It so happens we're going to Paris ourselves.

Scene Three
Drab Government Office

[MUSIC NO. 05B "THE RUMORS NEVER END"]

(The room is dominated by the Soviet flag and a picture of Lenin. Soviet bureaucracy did the decorating. It's hard to tell the men from the women in their drab office wear. They are sort of working but doing a lot more gossiping. Clearly, their superior is out of the room.)

WOMEN.

ANOTHER RUMOR
ON THE STREET.

MEN.

ANOTHER RUMOR TO
ATTEND

FILL OUT
A NEW REPORT
THE RUMORS
NEVER END.

THE RUMORS
NEVER END.

ANOTHER SCHEME,
ANOTHER LIE

SOLO.

ANOTHER SPY BETRAYS
A FRIEND

WOMEN.

FILL OUT
A NEW REPORT

THE RUMORS
NEVER END.

MEN.

FILL OUT
A NEW REPORT

THE RUMORS
NEVER END.

*(**GLEB VAGANOV** enters the room trailed by*

THREE WOMEN. *At the sight of him, everyone goes silent and makes a great show of going back to work. With* **GLEB** *are the three "failed" Anastasias:* **MARFA, DUNYA,** *and* **PAULINA.***)*

GLEB. Anything concerning the Romanovs, even the most preposterous rumor, we take very seriously.

DUNYA. *(To the other two.)* I *told* you.

PAULINA. *(To* **GLEB.***)* She's about as much a Romanov as I am.

MARFA. She's a streetsweeper. She was sleeping under a bridge until she took up with them.

PAULINA. Her name is Anya.

GLEB. Thank you.

DUNYA. Aren't you going to arrest them?

GLEB. You've done your duty. And I've done mine, listening to your gossip.

MARFA. It's not gossip. It's the truth.

*(***GLEB** *slams on desk.)*

GLEB. The next time I see the three of you soliciting on Theatre Street, I won't look the other way. Off with you.

(They go.)

ANOTHER RUMOR ON THE STREET.
ANOTHER GIRL TO APPREHEND.
ONE MORE PRETENDER
WHO'LL NO LONGER PLAY PRETEND.
FILL OUT A NEW REPORT.
THE RUMORS NEVER END.

ENSEMBLE.

FILL OUT A NEW REPORT

GLEB & ENSEMBLE.

THE RUMORS NEVER END...

ENSEMBLE.

THE RUMORS NEVER END...

Scene Four
The Yusupov Palace, Various Rooms

(The process of transforming **ANYA** *into Anastasia has begun.* **VLAD** *is the teacher;* **ANYA** *the student;* **DMITRY** *the occasionally impatient observer.)*

DMITRY. Are you ready to become the Grand Duchess Anastasia Nikolaevna Romanov?

ANYA. I'm ready to find out who I am but I'm not going to lie to do it.

DMITRY. It won't be a lie. We're going to help you remember the truth.

ANYA. I wish I had your confidence.

DMITRY. If the Dowager Empress recognizes you as her granddaughter, Vlad and I will get a small reward for our efforts and we'll all live happily ever after.

ANYA. And if she calls me an impostor?

DMITRY. It will just be an honest mistake. Either way, it gets you to Paris and us out of Russia. Everybody wins.

ANYA. How do you become the person you've forgotten you ever were?

[MUSIC NO. 06 "LEARN TO DO IT"]

VLAD. Take a deep breath, close your eyes and imagine another time, another world.

YOU WERE BORN
IN A PALACE BY THE SEA.

DMITRY. *(Reiterates.)*

A PALACE BY THE SEA.

ANYA.

COULD IT BE?

VLAD.

YES, IT'S SO.
YOU RODE HORSEBACK
WHEN YOU WERE ONLY THREE

ANYA. *(Spoken in rhythm.)*
    HORSEBACK RIDING? ME?

DMITRY.
    HORSE'S NAME?

VLAD.
    ROMEO!
    YOU THREW TANTRUMS
    AND TERRORIZED THE COOK!
    HOW THE PALACE SHOOK!

DMITRY.
    CHARMING CHILD!

VLAD.
    WROTE THE BOOK!
    BUT YOU'D BEHAVE
    WHEN YOUR FATHER GAVE THAT LOOK!

DMITRY.
    IMAGINE HOW IT WAS.
    YOUR LONG-FORGOTTEN PAST!

DMITRY & VLAD.
    WE'VE LOTS AND LOTS TO TEACH YOU
    AND THE TIME IS GOING FAST!

VLAD. Let's see you walk. Head up. Regal bearing.

    NOW, SHOULDERS BACK AND STAND UP TALL
    AND DO NOT WALK, BUT TRY TO FLOAT.

ANYA.
    I FEEL A LITTLE FOOLISH.
    (Spoken in rhythm.) AM I FLOATING?

DMITRY.
    LIKE A SINKING BOAT!

VLAD.
    YOU GIVE A BOW.

ANYA.
    WHAT HAPPENS NOW?

VLAD.
    YOUR HAND RECEIVES A KISS!

VLAD & DMITRY.

MOST OF ALL REMEMBER THIS:

VLAD.

IF I CAN LEARN TO DO IT,

YOU CAN LEARN TO DO IT.

DMITRY.

SOMETHING IN YOU KNOWS IT –

DMITRY & VLAD.

THERE'S NOTHING TO IT!

VLAD.

FOLLOW IN MY FOOTSTEPS,

SHOE BY SHOE!

VLAD & DMITRY.

YOU CAN LEARN TO DO IT TOO!

("Passage Of Time Music" as **ANYA** *becomes visibly weary.)*

ANYA. You're the ones who don't stand straight.

DMITRY. It's all his years of bowing and kowtowing at court.

VLAD. Bowing is a sign of respect.

DMITRY. I bowed to someone once.

VLAD. There, you admit it!

DMITRY. I was a boy, I didn't know any better. It was the first and last time.

*(***ANYA** *executes a flawless and very deep curtsey.)*

Where did you learn that?

VLAD. I didn't teach her. She's a natural. Be seated, young lady.

*(***VLAD** *draws a chair for her at a table.)*

DMITRY. NOW, ELBOWS IN AND SIT UP STRAIGHT

AND DO NOT SLURP THE STROGANOFF.

ANYA. *(Spoken in rhythm.)*

I NEVER CARED FOR STROGANOFF.

VLAD.

SHE SAID THAT LIKE A ROMANOV!

DMITRY.
> THE SAMOVAR!

VLAD.
> THE CAVIAR!

ANYA.
> DESSERT
> And then, goodnight?

DMITRY & VLAD.
> NOT UNTIL YOU GET THIS RIGHT!

VLAD.	**DMITRY.**
IF I CAN LEARN TO DO IT	IF HE CAN LEARN TO DO IT,
YOU CAN LEARN TO DO IT!	YOU CAN LEARN TO DO IT!
PULL YOURSELF TOGETHER	

VLAD & DMITRY.
> AND YOU'LL PULL THROUGH IT!

VLAD.
> TELL YOURSELF IT'S EASY

VLAD & DMITRY.
> AND IT'S TRUE!
> YOU CAN LEARN TO DO IT TOO!

> *(There is a passage of time, during which* **ANYA** *drills facts.)*

VLAD. Who is your great-grandmother?

ANYA. Queen Victoria.

VLAD. Great-great-grandmother?

ANYA. Princess Victoria of Saxe-Coburg-Saalfeld.

VLAD. Your best friend is...

ANYA. My little brother, Alexei.

DMITRY. Wrong! Your best friend is –

ANYA. I know who my best friend is!

DMITRY. What a temper.

ANYA. I don't like being contradicted.

DMITRY. That makes two of us!

VLAD. Continuing on…

    *(**DMITRY** hits the blackboard.)*

    NOW, HERE'S YOUR GREAT AUNT OLGA

DMITRY.

    HOW SHE FROLICKED ON THE VOLGA!

ANYA. Oh!

VLAD.

    YOUR DISTANT COUSIN VANYA.

    LOVED HIS VODKA!

DMITRY.

    GOT IT ANYA?

ANYA. *(Trying to scribble notes frantically.)* No!

VLAD.

    THE DUKE OF OLDENBURG WAS SHORT!

DMITRY.

    LOUISE OF BADEN

ANYA.

    HAD A…

DMITRY.

    WART!

VLAD.

    COUNT SERGEI

DMITRY.

    WORE A FEATHERED HAT.

VLAD.

    I HEAR HE'S GOTTEN VERY FAT!

ANYA.

    AND I RECALL HIS YELLOW CAT!

VLAD. I don't believe we told her that.

ANYA. *(Proudly.)*

    IF YOU CAN LEARN TO DO IT,

    I CAN LEARN TO DO IT!

VLAD.

    SAW YOU AND I KNEW IT!

ANYA.

> I'M GLAD YOU KNEW IT!
> SUDDENLY I FEEL LIKE
> THERE'S A CHANCE...

VLAD.

> NOT UNTIL YOU LEARN TO DANCE!

> *(**DMITRY** and **ANYA** are shy and resistant.)*

> *(They dance awkwardly, stumble...get better and better...)*

> WE HAVE ONLY JUST BEGUN!

VLAD & DMITRY.   **ANYA.**

> IF YOU CAN LEARN TO DO   IF I CAN LEARN TO DO IT,
>   IT,
> HE CAN LEARN TO DO IT!   YOU CAN LEARN TO DO IT!
> PULL YOURSELF
>   TOGETHER

VLAD, DMITRY & ANYA.

> AND WE'LL PULL THROUGH IT!

VLAD.

> TELL YOURSELF IT'S EASY,

VLAD, DMITRY & ANYA.

> AND IT'S TRUE!

VLAD & DMITRY.

> YOU CAN LEARN TO DO IT!

ANYA.

> NOTHING TO IT!

VLAD, DMITRY & ANYA.

> YOU CAN LEARN TO DO IT!

ANYA. *(Rapid fire, with confidence. Spoken in rhythm.)*

> THE CAVIAR. THE STROGANOFF.
> THE SAMOVAR. THE FEATHERED HAT.
> THE COUSIN DRANK, THE DUKE WAS SHORT.
> AND HERE A WART AND THERE A CAT.
> THE HORSE'S NAME WAS ROMEO.
> SO TELL ME SOMETHING NEW!

DMITRY & VLAD. *(Spoken in rhythm.)*

HA!

ANYA. *(Spoken in rhythm.)*

HA!

VLAD, DMITRY & ANYA.

YOU CAN LEARN TO DO IT, TOO!!

[MUSIC NO. 06A "LEARN TO DO IT (REPRISE)"]

VLAD. *Très bien, mademoiselle, très bien.*

ANYA. *Merci, monsieur, merci.*

VLAD. *Vous parlez français?*

ANYA. *(Surprising herself.) Un peu.*

VLAD. *(To* **DMITRY.***)* She's charming.

DMITRY. What were you telling her?

VLAD. The aristocrats all spoke French, Dmitry. Russian was for common people like you.

(To **ANYA.***)* You get to sleep on the sack of lentils tonight, Anya, you've earned it. *Bonne nuit, ma chère.* Tomorrow we begin again.

DMITRY. *(Stung.)* In *Russian,* for the common man.

*(***VLAD** *and* **DMITRY** *exit, leaving* **ANYA** *alone for a moment.)*

ANYA.

YOU WERE BORN IN A PALACE BY THE SEA.

COULD IT BE? ...

Scene Five
A Drab Government Office

> (**GLEB** *is on the telephone with his superior.*
> *He has an office to himself now. It has a view*
> *and his own telephone. He is well on his way*
> *up the Soviet ladder in his new uniform and*
> *boots and he is very pleased about it.*)

GLEB. Thank you, sir, your confidence in me will be justified: my own office with a view of the Nevsky Prospekt, a Russian telephone that works.

> (*His superior is not amused.*)

That was a joke. We have wonderful telephones.

> (*The door opens. An* **ASSISTANT** *pops his head in.*)

COMRADE #3. She's here.

> (*He goes.*)

GLEB. Sir, our little troublemaker has been found.

> (*He hangs up and goes to the window and*
> *stands looking down at the city below. He*
> *cuts a formidable figure with only his back*
> *for his visitor to ponder.* **ANYA** *enters.*)

It's a remarkable city, our Leningrad. All those people down there, coming and going, creating a future for themselves. I stand at this window for hours admiring them and wondering why a few bad apples are getting up to mischief instead. I can see all the way to the old Yusupov palace. Funny business going on there. Counter-revolutionary behavior some would say.

ANYA. Why was I brought here?

GLEB. I thought you could tell me, comrade.

> (*He turns to her.*)

You, the frightened little streetsweeper! I'd almost stopped looking for you on the Nevsky Prospekt. Anya? Am I right?

ANYA. Yes.

GLEB. I am Deputy Commissioner Gleb Vaganov. It's the uniform and the office that make the bad impression. I'm really not so bad. See? I have a sense of humor. You're shivering again. A friendly cup of tea will warm us both up.

ANYA. What is the charge?

GLEB. There is no charge. Why should there be? You have a job, food on the table, your own place in the new order of things.

ANYA. I'm very thankful.

GLEB. Which is why I'm warning you to leave your world of make-believe before it's too late.

ANYA. I don't understand.

GLEB. If you really were who you're pretending to be, they would kill you without hesitation.

ANYA. Everyone imagines being someone else. I'm no different. It's an innocent enough fantasy.

GLEB. No, Anya, a dangerous one. The Romanovs are gone, every last one of them. They no longer exist. My father was one of their guards.

ANYA. I don't want to hear this.

GLEB. When he was told to fire, he obeyed orders.

[MUSIC NO. 07 "THE NEVA FLOWS"]

BE VERY CAREFUL
OF THESE RUMORS THAT PREVAIL.
BE VERY CAREFUL WHAT YOU SAY.
I WAS A BOY
WHO LIVED THE TRUTH BEHIND THE TALE –
AND NO ONE GOT AWAY...

I SAW THE CHILDREN
AS THE SOLDIERS CLOSED THE GATE.
THE YOUNGEST DAUGHTER, AND HER PRIDE.
MY FATHER LEAVING,
ON THE NIGHT THEY MET THEIR FATE,
HIS PISTOL BY HIS SIDE.

THE NEVA FLOWS,
A NEW WIND BLOWS,
AND SOON IT WILL BE SPRING.
THE LEAVES UNFOLD
THE TSAR LIES COLD.
A REVOLUTION IS A SIMPLE THING...

I heard the shots, I heard their screams, but it's the silence after I remember most.

THE WORLD STOPPED BREATHING
AND I WAS NO LONGER A BOY...

MY FATHER SHOOK HIS HEAD
AND TOLD ME NOT TO ASK.
MY MOTHER SAID HE DIED OF SHAME.
BUT I BELIEVE HE DID A PROUD AND VITAL TASK
AND IN MY FATHER'S NAME...
THE NEVA FLOWS,

GLEB & ANYA. (**ANYA**, *unwillingly.*)

A NEW WIND BLOWS,
AND SOON IT WILL BE SPRING.
THE LEAVES UNFOLD.

GLEB.

THE TSAR LIES COLD.
(*Small, almost to himself.*) COULD I HAVE PULLED THE TRIGGER
IF I'D BEEN TOLD?
BE CAREFUL WHAT A DREAM MAY BRING.
A REVOLUTION IS A SIMPLE THING.

[MUSIC NO. 07A "SCENE & TRANSITION AFTER THE NEVA FLOWS"]

ANYA. Thank you for your warning, comrade.

GLEB. As your new friend, be careful, Anya. As Deputy Commissioner Gleb Vaganov, be very careful.

(**ANYA** *hurries off.* **GLEB** *stares after her.*)

I SAW THE CHILDREN
AS THE SOLDIERS CLOSED THE GATE...
ANYA...

Scene Six
A Park on the Banks of the Neva, at Night

[MUSIC NO. 08 "THE NEVA FLOWS (REPRISE)"]

(A crowd of Petersburg low-lifes is sharing a bottle of vodka to stave off the cold. They warm their hands over a fire. It's a cold night. They are "friends" of **DMITRY**.*)*

DRUNK #1. Life is good.

DRUNK #2. As long as there's vodka, life is wonderful.

DRUNK #3. I'll drink to that.

THE NEVA FLOWS,
A NEW WIND BLOWS,

DRUNK #1.

AND WHAT'S THAT AWFUL SMELL?

DRUNKS #2 & #4.

THE LEAVES UNFOLD,
THE TSAR LIES COLD...

ALL.

NOW HE'S DRINKING HIS VODKA IN HELL!

(Shouting and laughter. **DMITRY** *and* **ANYA** *pass.)*

ANYA. They know where we're living. His name is Gleb.

DRUNK #1. Look who's here, the Prince of Petersburg!

DRUNK #2. Thought you were in Paris.

DRUNK #1. He missed his old partners in crime.

DRUNK #3. Looks like he got himself a new girlfriend instead.

DMITRY. She's not my girlfriend.

DRUNK #4. If you don't want her, Dmitry, I'll take her. You want to dance, sweetheart?

DMITRY. Leave her alone!

(Fight ensues. Together, **ANYA** *and* **DMITRY**

rout the others. **ANYA***'s more than a tomboy.*
She has a feral ferocity about her when it
comes to defending herself from unwanted
attention. **ANYA** *stands ready to swing a big*
stick she has picked up as she yells after the
ruffians now in full retreat.)

ANYA. Next time I won't go so easy!

DMITRY. Where did you learn that? You're good.

ANYA. *(To* **DMITRY**, *half playfully.)* You want to see what
else I can do? Come at me. I won't hurt you.

DMITRY. *(Half-laughing; half convinced.)* I believe you!

ANYA. I didn't walk halfway across Russia without learning
how to take care of myself. You've had it easy.

DMITRY. Not so easy. My father was an anarchist. He died
in a labor camp for his convictions. My mother was
already gone. I don't really remember her.

ANYA. Who raised you then?

DMITRY. No one.

[MUSIC NO. 09 "MY PETERSBURG"]

I raised myself.

I GREW UP ON THE SLY,
IN THE GUTTERS AND THE STREETS
OF PETERSBURG.
JUST A KID ON THE FLY
GETTING GOOD AT GETTING BY
IN PETERSBURG!
I'VE BARTERED FOR A BLANKET,
STOLEN FOR MY BREAD.
LEARNED TO TAKE MY CHANCES
AND USE MY HEAD.
A RUSSIAN RAT IS CLEVER,
CLEVER OR HE ENDS UP DEAD!
BOILS DOWN TO:
THERE ARE SOME
WHO SURVIVE,
SOME WHO DON'T.

SOME GIVE UP.
SOME GIVE IN.
ME, I WON'T!
BLACK AND BLUE –
WELCOME TO
MY PETERSBURG.

Come, Anya!

(They start to move.)

STANDING HERE, YOU CAN SEE
FROM THE SPIRES TO THE PIERS
OF PETERSBURG!
I'D BE DOWN ON THAT QUAY*
SELLING STOLEN SOUVENIRS
OF PETERSBURG!
THE PALACES ABOVE AND
ALLEYWAYS BELOW.
FUNNY WHEN A CITY
IS ALL YOU KNOW –
HOW EVEN WHEN YOU HATE IT,
SOMETHING IN YOU LOVES IT SO!
THAT'S WHERE I
LEARNED MY STUFF
IN SOME ROUGH
COMPANY!
THERE'S THE BOY
GROWING UP
WHO WAS ME.
ALL I'VE BEEN
ALL I'LL BE...

WE CAN DO WHAT WE'RE TOLD,
WE CAN GO WHERE WE'RE LED.
BUT I LEARNED FROM MY FATHER
TO SEE WHAT'S AHEAD.
NOTHING HERE TO HOLD ME.
NO ONE THAT I OWE.
FUNNY HOW A BOY CAN GROW.
FUNNY HOW A CITY

---

* Pronounced "Key."

TELLS YOU WHEN IT'S TIME TO GO!

BOILS DOWN TO:
THERE ARE SOME
WHO HAVE WALLS
YET TO CLIMB!

DMITRY & ANYA.

YOU AND I,
ON THE FLY,
JUST IN TIME!

DMITRY.

BUT TONIGHT
THERE'S A SKY
AND QUITE A VIEW...

WELCOME TO...
MY PETERSBURG!

Scene Seven
Same Park

(Only now its grand view of the river is revealed.)

DMITRY. My father used to bring me here. He'd put me on his shoulders so I could have a better view. "Bet you can see all the way to Finland from up there, Dima!"

ANYA. Dima.

DMITRY. That's what he called me. There isn't a day I don't miss him.

ANYA. So neither of us has a family.

DMITRY. You don't know that yet. The answer is in Paris.

> *(Breaking an awkward moment by going back to her "Anastasia lessons.")*

Now, tell me about her little dog.

ANYA. His name was Toby.

> *(She falters at the memory.)*

DMITRY. Go on.

ANYA. I loved him so much.

DMITRY. Don't stop.

ANYA. I'm not as strong as you think I am!

> *(**DMITRY** reaches into his satchel.)*

DMITRY. Close your eyes.

ANYA. Why?

DMITRY. Just do it. Put your hand out.

> *(**ANYA** closes her eyes and puts her hand out.)*

Open. You've worked hard. You've earned it.

ANYA. What is it?

> *(It is the music box from the Prologue. It looks very battered.)*

DMITRY. A music box.

ANYA. It's beautiful.

DMITRY. It's broken. I can't even open it.

[MUSIC NO. 10 "ONCE UPON A DECEMBER (ENSEMBLE)"]

(**ANYA** *easily opens it, winds it, and it begins to play. We will hear a familiar tune. Only this time perhaps some of the notes don't sound properly or they are out of tune. No matter,* **ANYA** *is entranced.*)

How did you do that? Anya?

(*But* **ANYA** *is transported into another world, another time.*)

ANYA.
DANCING BEARS,
PAINTED WINGS,
THINGS I ALMOST REMEMBER.
AND A SONG SOMEONE SINGS
ONCE UPON A DECEMBER.
SOMEONE HOLDS ME SAFE AND WARM.
HORSES PRANCE THROUGH A SILVER STORM.
FIGURES DANCING GRACEFULLY
ACROSS MY MEMORY...

RUSSIAN CHORUS.
AH...

(*Through them weave the royal family... as they were once upon a time. They waltz gloriously, as if at a ball in 1906.*)

ANYA.
SOMEONE HOLDS ME SAFE AND WARM.
HORSES PRANCE THROUGH A SILVER STORM.
FIGURES DANCING GRACEFULLY

ANYA.	**RUSSIAN CHORUS.**
ACROSS MY MEMORY...	AH...
FAR AWAY, LONG AGO,	AH...
GLOWING DIM AS AN EMBER,	AH...

ANYA.	RUSSIAN CHORUS.
THINGS MY HEART USED TO KNOW	AH...
THINGS IT YEARNS TO REMEMBER	AH...
AND A SONG SOMEONE SINGS ONCE UPON A DECEMBER.	

ANYA. How soon do you think we can go? They're canceling trains right and left. Here, I worked an extra shift this week.

> *(She hands him some rubles.)*

It's not much but every little bit helps.

DMITRY. We're not even close, Anya.

ANYA. What are you saying?

DMITRY. I thought I could get us out before they closed the borders for good.

ANYA. You were the only hope I had.

DMITRY. There must be someone who can help you. I'm sorry.

> *(He hands her rubles back.)*

ANYA. I don't want your money.

DMITRY. It's your money.

ANYA. It's our money. I trusted you.

DMITRY. I said I was sorry!

ANYA. But I didn't trust you enough. Now you close *your* eyes.

DMITRY. What for?

ANYA. You're the stubbornest person I ever met, almost as stubborn as me.

> *(**DMITRY** closes his eyes.)*

Put your hand out.

> *(**ANYA** puts something in **DMITRY**'s open palm.)*

All right, open.

> (**DMITRY** *opens his eyes.*)

[MUSIC NO. 10A "A SECRET SHE KEPT"]

DMITRY. It's a diamond.

ANYA. A nurse at the hospital found it sewn in my underclothes.

SHE HID IT FOR ME
TILL THE DAY I COULD GO.
A SECRET SHE KEPT,
ALTHOUGH WHY, I DON'T KNOW.
SHE SAID, "DON'T TELL A SOUL
TILL THE MOMENT YOU MUST."
I HAD TO MAKE SURE I FOUND
SOMEONE I TRUST...

DMITRY. You've had it all this time without telling me?

ANYA. Yes.

DMITRY. Why?

ANYA. It's the only thing I have. Without it, I have nothing.

DMITRY. How do you know I won't take it now and you'll never see me again?

ANYA. I don't think you will.

DMITRY. If you weren't a girl, I'd –

> (*Instead he hugs* **ANYA** *tightly and kisses her on both cheeks. She's not accustomed to such spontaneous expressions of emotions, especially coming from such a roughneck as* **DMITRY. VLAD** *enters with great urgency.*)

[MUSIC NO. 10B "VLAD UNDERSCORE / TRANSITION TO TRAIN STATION"]

VLAD. Disaster! The Yusupov Palace has been raided. We're done for if we go back there.

> (**DMITRY** *has produced the diamond.* **VLAD***'s eyes grow large.*)

Mother of Moses!

DMITRY. She had it all along.

ANYA. I didn't trust either of you with it.

VLAD. I don't blame you, but never mind, all is forgiven, I love you, Anya.

DMITRY. Vlad, I'm trusting you to get the exit papers.

VLAD. Done.

(He rushes off.)

ANYA. Hurry, there's a train at midnight from the Finland Station!

DMITRY. I'll fence the diamond. Where are you going?

ANYA. They owe me a week's wages. Every ruble counts.

(She rushes off.)

DMITRY. We're going to Paris on a train. I'm going to sleep in a hotel and take a bath in a real bathtub.

(They have all rushed off in the opposite directions as we transition to:)

Scene Eight
A Train Station in St. Petersburg

(It is teeming with people anxious to leave Russia. There are all kinds: old, young, rich, poor, healthy, sick. The only thing they have in common is their desperation to leave. There are probably some nobility among them but they are in disguise.)

(ANYA and DMITRY enter with their few belongings in a suitcase and some burlap bags.)

ANNOUNCER. Train for Budapest on Track Four. Paris via Budapest on Track Four.

(VLAD enters with ANYA and DMITRY.)

VLAD. It's a special train. Aristocrats and intellectuals: everyone the Bolsheviks want to be rid of. We will be traveling as members of the Diaghilev Ballets Russes. They've taken Paris by storm.

(A MAN starts at the sight of ANYA. He quickly comes over to her and kisses her hand. Just as quickly he darts away and disappears into the crowd.)

COUNT IPOLITOV. God bless you.

VLAD. I recognize that man. He's the Count Ipolitov. He's not just an aristocrat but an intellectual as well. He's a dead man on both counts.

ANNOUNCER. Train for Budapest on Track Four. Paris via Budapest on Track Four. All aboard!

VLAD. We should go.

[MUSIC NO. 11 "STAY, I PRAY YOU"]

(But no one moves. It is as if they are all frozen. They each realize – rich, poor, old, young, etc. – that this is probably the last

*time they will see their beloved St. Petersburg
or ever be in Russia again.)*

COUNT IPOLITOV.

HOW CAN I DESERT YOU?
HOW TO TELL YOU WHY?
COACHMAN, HOLD THE HORSES,
STAY, I PRAY YOU.
LET ME HAVE A MOMENT.
LET ME SAY GOODBYE

                    MEN & WOMEN.

TO BRIDGE AND RIVER,	*(Hums.)*
FOREST AND WATERFALL	*(Hums.)*
ORCHARD, SEA, AND SKY.	*(Hums.)*
HARSH AND SWEET	AH
AND BITTER TO LEAVE IT ALL	AH

COUNT IPOLITOV, MEN & WOMEN.

I'LL BLESS MY HOMELAND TILL I DIE.
HOW TO BREAK THE TIE?
WE HAVE SHED OUR TEARS
AND SHARED OUR SORROWS.
THOUGH THE SCARS REMAIN AND
TEARS WILL NEVER DRY...
I'LL BLESS MY HOMELAND TILL I DIE...

ANYA.

NEVER TO RETURN,

DMITRY.

FIN'LLY BREAKING FREE

ANYA & DMITRY.

YOU ARE ALL I KNOW.
YOU HAVE RAISED ME.

VLAD.

HOW TO TURN AWAY?
HOW TO CLOSE THE DOOR?

ANYA, DMITRY & VLAD.

HOW TO GO WHERE I
HAVE NEVER GONE BEFORE...

ALL.

HOW CAN I DESERT YOU?
HOW TO TELL YOU WHY?
COACHMAN, HOLD THE HORSES,
STAY, I PRAY YOU.
LET ME HAVE A MOMENT.
LET ME SAY GOODBYE

(People begin to board the train.)

COUNT IPOLITOV.	**MEN & WOMEN.**
AH AH AH	*(Hums.)*
	AH

ALL.

HARSH AND SWEET
AND BITTER TO LEAVE IT ALL
I'LL BLESS MY HOMELAND TILL I DIE.

(The singing diminishes as more and more go.)

ANYA, DMITRY & VLAD.

I'LL BLESS MY HOMELAND...

(VLAD begins to leave.)

ANYA & DMITRY.

I'LL BLESS MY HOMELAND...

(Finally only ANYA is left.)

ANYA.

I'LL BLESS MY HOMELAND TILL I DIE.

Scene Nine
A Train Compartment

(ANYA is reading. DMITRY and VLAD in conversation. They are sharing the compartment with quite a few other people. It's been a long day. They show it.)

[MUSIC NO. 12 "WE'LL GO FROM THERE"]

VLAD. *(Indignant.)* This is outrageous. I paid for first-class. We should be having champagne and caviar.

DMITRY. *(Approvingly.)* There is no more first-class. Everyone is equal now.

VLAD. *(With some admiration.)* You don't have to sound so damn happy about it.

(A SMOKER strikes a match.)

ANYA. How dare you smoke without my permission?

SMOKER. Who the hell do you think you are?

ANYA. I am the Grand Duchess Anastasia Romanov.

SMOKER. I'm in a compartment with a crazy woman!

(He gets up and leaves the car.)

DMITRY. Warn us next time before you do that!

ANYA. I wanted to see what it felt like, saying I was her.

VLAD. It's a long trip. You have plenty of time to practice. In Paris, your first challenge will be the Dowager Empress's lady-in-waiting, Lily, the Countess Malevsky-Malevitch. No one has access to Her Majesty without her.

DMITRY. She sounds like a dragon.

VLAD. Quite the opposite. Lily was beautiful, voluptuous, married – everything I look for in a woman. She gave me a watch studded with diamonds.

ANYA. Did you love her?

VLAD. Madly, darling. But I loved the watch more.

*(Shaking her head at the two men, **ANYA** goes*

back to her book.)

DMITRY. What happened to it?

VLAD. Gone with the old Russia, like everything else. I hope Lily's happy to see me.

(To himself, preening but insecure.) Be honest, Vlad Popov, how could she not be?

I MAY HAVE GOTTEN FATTER,
BUT MAYBE THAT WON'T MATTER.
BOTTOM LINE... I'LL WIN HER.

WE'LL DO SOME REMINISCING.
SHE'LL SEE WHAT SHE'S BEEN MISSING
OVER WINE...
AND DINNER!

AND THOUGH I KNOW I'VE GROWN A TINY BIT GRAY,
SOME WOMEN SAY I LOOK DISTINGUISHED THIS WAY.
I'LL BOW AS IF I'M STILL A FRISKY YOUNG PUP.
LET'S HOPE THAT I CAN STRAIGHTEN UP!
IF SHE SAYS NO
WE'LL ALL LAY LOW
AND WE'LL GO FROM THERE!

*(The train spins, revealing **ANYA**.)*

ANYA.

HANDS SHAKING.
HEART THUND'RING!
MEET THE ROYAL... MESS!
START SMILING.
STOP WOND'RING:
WHY DID I SAY... YES?

*(The train spins, overlapping lines, to reveal **DMITRY**.)*

ANYA & DMITRY.

THIS CHANCE IS ALL I'VE GOT.

(Spin lands on this line.)

DMITRY.

KEEP A GRIP AND TAKE A DEEP BREATH AND

SOON WE'LL KNOW WHAT'S WHAT...
PUT ON OUR SHOW,
REWARDS WILL FLOW
AND WE'LL GO FROM THERE!

ANYA.
AND WE'LL GO
FROM THERE

VLAD.
AND WE'LL GO
FROM THERE

ANYA, VLAD & DMITRY.
AND WE'LL GO FROM THERE!

ALL.
OH, WHAT A LOVELY RIDE
AND WHAT A LOVELY DAY

DMITRY, VLAD & ANYA.
FOR A TOTALLY ILLEGAL

ALL.
LOVELY GETAWAY!

VLAD.	DMITRY.	ANYA.
I MAY HAVE		HANDS
GOTTEN FATTER	HANDS	SHAKING
BUT MAYBE	SHAKING	HEART
THAT WON'T		THUND'RING
MATTER		
BOTTOM LINE:	MEET THE	MEET THE
	ROYAL	ROYAL
I'LL	MESS!	MESS!
WIN HER		
WE'LL DO SOME		START
REMINISCING	START	SMILING
SHE'LL SEE WHAT	SMILING	STOP
SHE'S BEEN		WOND'RING
MISSING		
OVER WINE	WHY DID I SAY	WHY DID I
		SAY

VLAD.	DMITRY.	ANYA.
AND	YES?	YES?
DINNER!		THIS
AND THOUGH I KNOW	THIS	CHANCE
I'VE GROWN A TINY BIT GRAY	CHANCE	IS
	IS	ALL
	ALL I'VE	I'VE
SOME WOMEN SAY I LOOK	GOT	GOT
DISTINGUISHED	KEEP A GRIP AND	KEEP A GRIP AND
THIS WAY	TAKE A DEEP BREATH AND	TAKE A DEEP BREATH AND
I'LL BOW AS IF		SOON
I'M STILL A	SOON WE'LL	WE'LL
FRISKY YOUNG PUP	KNOW WHAT'S	KNOW WHAT'S
LET'S HOPE THAT I CAN STRAIGHTEN UP!	WHAT...	WHAT...

(Pulls himself together.)
BUT NO MORE
DOUBT!

DMITRY.
NO TIME TO SPARE!

ANYA.
WE'RE NEARLY
OUT!

ANYA, VLAD & DMITRY.
SO LET'S PREPARE!

ANYA, VLAD, DMITRY & TRAIN RIDERS.
WE'RE ON OUR WAY
TO WHO KNOWS WHERE!

ANYA, VLAD & DMITRY.
AND WE'LL GO
MALE TRAIN RIDERS.
AND WE'LL GO
FEMALE TRAIN RIDERS.
AND WE'LL GO
ANYA, VLAD, DMITRY & TRAIN RIDERS.
FROM THERE!
ANYA, VLAD & DMITRY. We'll go from there!

> *(There is a sharp knock on the compartment door. Two* **POLICE** *enter.)*

POLICEMAN #1. Papers. Papers.

VLAD. Good evening, gentlemen. Is there a problem?

POLICEMAN #1. We're looking for someone who is illegally leaving the country.

VLAD. Didn't have the right papers, eh?

POLICEMAN #2. He had the right papers; he had the wrong name. Count Ipolitov.

> *(There is the sound of a loud gunshot. The* **POLICE** *rush off. Our three travelers know what has happened.* **ANYA** *makes the sign of the cross.* **VLAD** *bows his head.)*

VLAD. I'll go see what happened.

DMITRY. We know what happened.

VLAD. Calm her down. Any tears will betray us.

> *(He goes.)*

DMITRY. We'll be safe soon.

ANYA. That's what the soldiers said but they were pointing guns at us.

DMITRY. No one's pointing guns at you. You're taking this too far, Anya.

ANYA. Not if I *am* really her!

DMITRY. Ssssh, shhh, we're almost out of Russia. Once we cross the border, we're safe.

ANYA. You put these ideas in my head and I'm beginning to think they might be true.

[MUSIC NO. 12A "JUMP!"]

(*VLAD bursts into the compartment.*)

VLAD. Three Chekist officers just came aboard with orders to arrest two men and a young woman.

DMITRY. That could be anyone.

VLAD. I don't think so.

(*VLAD holds up a wanted poster. The three of them are on it!*)

DMITRY. What are we going to do?

ANYA. We're getting off.

VLAD. The train's moving again.

ANYA. Unless you want to end up like Count Ipolitov.

VLAD, DMITRY & ANYA. Jump!!

Scene Ten
Gleb's Office in St. Petersburg /
Various Places on the Road

(**GLEB** *is with his superior, an enraged* **GORLINSKY**.)

[MUSIC NO. 14 "TRAVELING SEQUENCE / STILL"]

GORLINSKY. The train crossed the Russian border and they weren't on it?

GLEB. *(Downplaying the fact that they lost her.)*
A TEMPORARY SETBACK.
WE'LL FIND THEM, NEVER FEAR.
THEY THINK THEY CAN ELUDE US
BUT THEY'LL END UP HERE.

GORLINSKY.
A RAGGED LITTLE UPSTART
ENGAGING IN A CRIME!

> *(A flash of lightning reveals our trio, hiking across Latvia / Lithuania. It's pouring with rain.)*

ANYA, VLAD, DMITRY, GLEB & GORLINSKY.
THE PRINCESS ANASTASIA
IS RUNNING OUT OF TIME!

> *(**VLAD** sits, panting from exhaustion.)*

VLAD. Dmitry, wait! Anya can't go any further, she's exhausted.

> *(Clearly **VLAD** is the only one of them who is.)*

DMITRY. The Polish border is only ten more kilometers. We'll be safe there.

VLAD. Wait for me!

> *(Lights up on the office again.)*

GORLINSKY. Follow her to Paris. If she's not Anastasia bring her back. We'll make an example of her.

GLEB. And if she is Anastasia?

GORLINSKY. Finish the job for your father, like a good son.

IT'S REALLY VERY SIMPLE.
YOU MERELY POINT THE GUN.
AND THEN YOU PULL THE TRIGGER

GLEB.

AND THE JOB IS DONE.

GORLINSKY.

ENJOY YOUR NEW POSITION.
THE TELEPHONE. THE VIEW.

GLEB & GORLINSKY.

THE PRINCESS ANASTASIA!

> *(Our trio crosses again, this time via another form of transportation – bicycles.)*

GORLINSKY.

ALIVE OR DEAD...
It's up to you.

> *(**GORLINSKY** goes. **GLEB** comes downstage, alone with himself.)*

GLEB. "Everyone imagines being someone else. It's an innocent enough fantasy."

> *(As he sings, he will be given an overcoat, passport, a suitcase, and a gun.)*

AN UNDERHANDED GIRL.
AN ACT OF DESPERATION.
AND TO MY CONSTERNATION
I LET HER GO.

SHE WANTS WHAT SHE CAN GET.
IS THAT A FAIR DEPICTION?
DOES SHE BELIEVE HER FICTION?
IT'S HARD TO KNOW.

IS IT INNOCENCE OR GUILE
OR NOTHING BUT A CHILDISH ACT OF WILL?
SHE DOESN'T KNOW SHE NEEDS YOU.
SHE WILLFULLY MISLEADS YOU,

BUT STILL...
STILL...

A SON BECOMES A MAN
AT HIS FATHER'S KNEE.
IF MY FATHER ASKED QUESTIONS
WELL, WHERE WOULD WE BE?

SHE'S NOTHING BUT A CHILD.
A WAIF WHO NEEDS PROTECTION.
I FEEL A STRANGE CONNECTION
I CAN'T ALLOW.

SHE SAYS IT'S ALL A GAME.
SHE TREMBLES LIKE A FLOWER
BUT IN HER, THERE'S A POWER.
I SEE THAT NOW...

I AM NOTHING BUT A MAN
WITH NOTHING BUT HIS ORDERS TO FULFILL.
"I'M INNOCENT," SHE CRIES.
BUT THEN YOU SEE HER EYES,
AND SOMETHING IN THEM TELLS YOU
THAT SHE ABSOLUTELY LIES!
UNTIL YOUR HEART REPLIES:
BUT STILL!
STILL!
STILL!

Scene Eleven
A Wide Open Country Space

(They look like they've been traveling for days and days.)

VLAD. *La belle France.*

DMITRY. It looks like Russia.

VLAD. France looks nothing like Russia. It looks like France. Open your hearts and minds to all this. Learn something. I'm getting emotional. The last time I was in Paris I was a young man. My waist was like this.

ANYA. Why have we stopped? I'm going to ask the driver what's wrong.

DMITRY. Look at her rattling off in French with him. You've taught her well. Don't be surprised if we get away with this, Vlad.

VLAD. She'll break your heart, Dmitry.

DMITRY. Be quiet, what do you know about anything?

VLAD. If they accept her as Anastasia, you'll never see her again.

DMITRY. As usual, you don't know what you're talking about.

     *(**ANYA** returns.)*

ANYA. This is as far as he goes but we're almost there. From the top of the hill, he says you can just see Paris.

[MUSIC NO. 14 "JOURNEY TO THE PAST"]

VLAD. Are you ready to be astonished?

     *(**VLAD** starts up the hill.)*

DMITRY. We made it!

ANYA. Even when I was mad at you, I never doubted we would. Thank you, Dmitry.

DMITRY. *(Deflecting her sincerity.)* Thank Vlad.

VLAD. *(From the crest.)* I can see the Eiffel Tower. It's true, it's really there.

(**DMITRY** *bounds up the hill like a young goat.*)

DMITRY. *(At the top.)* Anya, come see!

(**DMITRY** *and* **VLAD** *stand on the crest of the hill looking down on Paris while* **ANYA** *hesitates.*)

Anya!

VLAD. Anya!

ANYA.

HEART, DON'T FAIL ME NOW.
COURAGE, DON'T DESERT ME!
DON'T TURN BACK NOW THAT WE'RE HERE.
PEOPLE ALWAYS SAY
LIFE IS FULL OF CHOICES.
NO ONE EVER MENTIONS FEAR,
OR HOW THE WORLD CAN SEEM SO VAST
ON A JOURNEY TO THE PAST...

SOMEWHERE DOWN THIS ROAD
I KNOW SOMEONE'S WAITING.
YEARS OF DREAMS JUST CAN'T BE WRONG.
ARMS WILL OPEN WIDE.
I'LL BE SAFE AND WANTED,
FIN'LLY HOME WHERE I BELONG
WELL, STARTING NOW I'M LEARNING FAST,
ON THIS JOURNEY TO THE PAST...

HOME, LOVE, FAM'LY.
THERE WAS ONCE A TIME
I MUST HAVE HAD THEM, TOO.
HOME, LOVE, FAM'LY.
I WILL NEVER BE COMPLETE
UNTIL I FIND YOU!

ONE STEP AT A TIME,
ONE HOPE, THEN ANOTHER,
WHO KNOWS WHERE THIS ROAD MAY GO?
BACK TO WHO I WAS.
ON TO FIND MY FUTURE.
THINGS MY HEART STILL NEEDS TO KNOW.
YES, LET THIS BE A SIGN!

LET THIS ROAD BE MINE!
LET IT LEAD ME TO MY PAST,
AND BRING ME HOME
AT LAST!

(She turns and follows them.)

End of Act I

ACT II

(An Entr'acte leads us to a colorful tableau.)

Scene One
We are on the Champs-Élysées

[MUSIC NO. 15 "PARIS HOLDS THE KEY"]

(In Paris. It is a bright, sunny spring day. Nothing could be further from the winter gloom of St. Petersburg when we first met **ANYA, DMITRY,** *and* **VLAD.***)*

(It is as if we have moved to another world, another century, another planet almost. People are well-dressed, cheerful, and confident that theirs is the best of all possible worlds.)

*(***ANYA, DMITRY,*** *and* **VLAD** *run on.* **VLAD** *stops short and reacts.)*

VLAD.
VOILÀ, MES AMIS! HERE'S PARIS!*
NOW THAT WE'RE HERE, FOLLOW ME!
BEGIN WITH THE VIEW
AS YOU STROLL DOWN "LA RUE"
PEOPLE OF PARIS.
AND SOON ALL PARIS
WILL BE SINGING TO YOU!
ALL.
OOH, OOH, AH, AH!

---

* Pronounced "Paree" here and throughout this song.

PEOPLE OF PARIS.

> PARIS HOLDS THE KEY TO YOUR HEART!
> AND ALL OF PARIS PLAYS A PART!
> PARIS TURNED A PAGE
> TO THE NEW MODERN AGE!

VLAD.

> AND WE'LL DO IT TOO, IF WE'RE SMART!

VLAD & PEOPLE OF PARIS.

> THE FRENCH HAVE IT DOWN TO AN ART!

PEOPLE OF PARIS.

> EVERYONE'S A WRITER! PAINTER! POET!
> EVERYTHING IS AVANT GARDE OR CHIC!

VLAD.

> WE'LL BE IN THE KNOW BEFORE WE KNOW IT!

ALL.

> WHEN YOU'RE IN THE KNOW, IT'S...
> OH, IT'S MAGNIFIQUE
> TO FIND IN PARIS WHAT YOU SEEK...

DMITRY.

> PARIS HOLDS THE KEY TO HER FATE.
> WE WON'T HAVE MUCH LONGER TO WAIT.
> AND THEN, COME WHAT MAY
> WE WILL EACH GO OUR WAY...

ANYA.

> I DREAMED OF A CITY BEYOND ALL COMPARE.
> IT'S HARD TO BELIEVE THAT I'M FINALLY THERE...

VLAD.

> AT LAST THERE'S A FUTURE

DMITRY.

> THERE'S FREEDOM

ANYA.

> THERE'S HOPE

ANYA, DMITRY & VLAD.

> IN THE AIR!

PEOPLE OF PARIS.

> AH AH

ALL.

AH
PARIS HOLDS THE KEY TO YOUR HEART!
THE PLEASURES OF LIFE À LA CARTE!
COME DANCE THROUGH THE NIGHT
AND FORGET ALL YOUR WOES!
THE CITY OF LIGHT!
HOW IT GLITTERS AND GLOWS!
AND ONE NEVER KNOWS WHAT WILL START!

(Transition to an elevator, going up and up.)

PARIS HOLDS THE KEY
TO YOUR...

(The elevator opens, spilling them all onto the observation deck.)

HEART!

(They look down over a bird's-eye view of Paris as fireworks explode.)

Scene Two
The Alexander Bridge

(The number ends on the Alexander Bridge. Everyone goes, leaving **ANYA** *suddenly alone on the bridge with her future at stake. The sun is going down on a magical day.)*

[MUSIC NO. 16 "PARIS HOLDS THE KEY (REPRISE)"]

DMITRY. I don't know about anyone else but it's been a long day. I'll be at the hotel.

VLAD. Don't use up all the hot water!

(To **ANYA**.*)* I've never seen him so happy. I'm going to try to find Lily. I'll start at the Neva Club.

(He goes. **ANYA** *is alone on the bridge with her thoughts.)*

ANYA. "Considered the most beautiful bridge in Paris, the Alexander Bridge, was named for Tsar Alexandre III."
PARIS* HOLDS THE KEY TO MY HEART
AND ALL OF PARIS PLAYS A PART.
THIS BRIDGE IS A GOOD PLACE TO START...

---

* Pronounced "Paree" in this song.

Scene Three
An Elegant Salon in a
Luxurious Parisian Town House

(Rented by **THE DOWAGER EMPRESS** *and her entourage.)*

*(***LILY** *is firmly showing* **COUNT LEOPOLD** *to the door. He is a foppish, dyed-hair, unctuous, distant relative of* **THE DOWAGER EMPRESS.**)*

LILY. I'm sorry, Count Leopold.

LEOPOLD. She can't always be resting! The Dowager Empress knows I have important papers for her to sign.

LILY. Papers designating *you* the heir to the Romanov fortune. She will never sign them.

LEOPOLD. She is an old woman who has outlived her place in history. Anastasia is a pathetic figment of her imagination. Eventually, I will be recognized as the sole beneficiary of the Tsar's estate by an international court of law.

LILY. I'll tell Her Majesty you called.

*(***LEOPOLD** *tries a different tactic.)*

LEOPOLD. You'll be at the Neva Club this evening, Lily?

LILY. Along with every other White Russian in Paris.

LEOPOLD. I will want the first Charleston.

LILY. I've given up dancing for Lent.

LEOPOLD. Lent just ended.

LILY. Next Lent, I'm getting an early start.

(She has succeeded in getting him out the door and firmly closing it. She picks up the day's mail and begins sorting it.)

THE DOWAGER EMPRESS. *(Offstage.)* Is he gone?

*(***THE DOWAGER EMPRESS** *enters. She is a deeply changed woman. She is older, obviously, but she is less invincible. Her heart has been*

*thoroughly broken. If she can show that side
of herself it will be to* **LILY** *and no one else.)*

LILY. Your Imperial Majesty.

THE DOWAGER EMPRESS. He's like a dog with a bone, that one.

LILY. Only four letters today.

THE DOWAGER EMPRESS. If only I could lose hope entirely. I used to open each one with a beating heart. Could this be my precious Anastasia? But after so many disappointments, I've come to dread the daily post. Another day, another impostor.

LILY. I won't let you give up.

THE DOWAGER EMPRESS. Dearest Lily. I know I am a proud and difficult woman. You are the only one I've allowed to see what's become of me. I was Maria Fyodorovna Romanov, Empress of All Russia. You can't possibly know what that means, Lily. No one can.

LILY. *(Reads, to cover her embarrassment.)* "Your Majesty, remember our happy summers by the sea in Livadia…"

THE DOWAGER EMPRESS. Livadia! They all do their homework.

LILY. "Strange and bizarre events have brought me to Buenos Aires. Bring me to Paris and I will convince you I am Anastasia."

THE DOWAGER EMPRESS. *(Dismissive.)* She wants me to pay her passage. At least that little impostor from Cleveland paid her own way. What is Cleveland? I never heard of such a place. It sounds dreadful. Cleveland!

LILY. *(A new letter.)* "Dearest Grandma*ma*, if I may call you that, Your Majesty –"

THE DOWAGER EMPRESS. I was never "Grandmama." I was "Nana." I was only "Nana."

"Grandmama"! They play me for a fool. Give me those.

*(She takes the letters and tries to destroy
them. She is too weak. She lets them fall.)*

No more letters, no more interviews.

LILY. There will be other young women. What shall I tell them?

THE DOWAGER EMPRESS. Tell them they're too late. The Grand Duchess Anastasia Romanov is dead and the Dowager Empress is dead with her. Leave me.

LILY. I'll light the lamps. Will you be all right this evening?

[MUSIC NO. 17 "CLOSE THE DOOR"]

THE DOWAGER EMPRESS. My precious Anastasia.

LILY. She doesn't hear me.

(She leaves **THE DOWAGER EMPRESS** *alone.)*

THE DOWAGER EMPRESS.
THESE STRANGERS
COME CALLING.
SOON ENOUGH THEY'RE GONE.
THE TWILIGHT
IS FALLING.
LAMPS WILL SOON GO ON.
AND WHERE DOES SUMMER GO?
I WILL NEVER KNOW.
SUMMER USED TO LAST ENDLESSLY.
CHILDREN ALL IN WHITE,
RUNNING DOWN THE SAND
TO ME...
TO ME...

I'VE BELIEVED SO LONG,
I HAVE DARED TO HOPE
THAT THE DOOR MIGHT OPEN
AND THAT YOU MIGHT ENTER.

> *(She looks at photographs and envisions Anastasia.)*

PLAYING HIDE AND SEEK.
KISSES ON MY CHEEK.

THE LAMPS BEGIN TO GLOW.
IN MY HEART, I KNOW
YOU'RE A LIE THAT I'VE WAITED FOR.

TELL THEM ALL TO GO.
TELL THEM ALL – NO MORE!
TELL THEM I CLOSE THE DOOR.

Scene Four
Outside the Neva Club

[MUSIC NO. 17A "UNDERSCORE BEFORE LAND OF YESTERDAY"]

(A luxurious, almost decadent, hideaway for White Russian aristocrats who have escaped their homeland and are trying to establish a resistance to the new order and maintain their old ways and familiar culture in Paris, their new – and they hope temporary – home. People in evening wear are arriving for dinner and dancing after a night at the theatre.)

*(They are familiar faces to the young Russian doorman (**SERGEI**).)*

*(**GLEB** appears. He is dressed as a civilian in decidedly non-fashionable, clunky Soviet style. His suit is poorly tailored; his shoes are all wrong.)*

SERGEI. Welcome to Paris, comrade.

GLEB. I beg your pardon?

SERGEI. Only just-off-the-train Russians wear shoes like yours. I had the same pair. Try the Russian tea shop on the Rue du Bac, Number Seventeen. Last I heard, they were hiring.

GLEB. I'm not looking for work, comrade.

> *(**LILY** enters.)*

SERGE. Good evening, Countess Lily.

LILY. The only thing good about it is that it means one day less. I'm being Russian, Sergei. I love life.

> *(**COUNT GREGORY** and his **WIFE** enter.)*

Count Gregory, how was the ballet?

COUNT GREGORY. Dreadful. You never heard such a racket.

Thank God for *Swan Lake* next week. *Real* Russian music, not this Stravinsky.

COUNTESS GREGORY. You'll be there, Lily, with her Imperial Majesty?

LILY. But of course. A lady-in-waiting's life is never her own.

COUNTESS GREGORY. Marvelous. I haven't seen The Dowager Empress since the Russian opera season.

(They exit into the Neva Club. **GLEB** *has overheard this information.)*

SERGE. Don't loiter, they won't like it. Go to the back door. Kostya will give you something to eat.

GLEB. I'd rather starve than eat their scraps. They make me ashamed to be Russian.

(He exits.)

Scene Four A
Inside the Neva Club

[MUSIC NO. 18 "LAND OF YESTERDAY"]

(Some people are dancing a desultory fox-trot or maybe a Charleston. Others are talking politics.)

EXILED RUSSIAN. Thank God for the Neva Club, St. Petersburg on the Seine.

LILY. Only a fool would go back. My husband was very sorry he did. Ten families were living in our ballroom alone. There were chickens in the wine cellar. It's not the Russia he remembered.

COUNT GREGORY. What is it our great poet said?

LEOPOLD. Which one? We have so many.

LILY. It doesn't matter. They all say the same thing. "Past glories, present griefs."
ONCE, I HAD A PALACE.
HERE, MERELY A FLAT.
I FLED WITH SOME DIAMONDS
AND THAT WAS THAT.

ARISTOCRATS.
IT'S VERY TRAGIC!

LILY.	**ARISTOCRATS.**
ONCE, LADIES-IN-WAITING	OOH
ALL BENDING A KNEE!	
NOW, ONLY ONE LADY-IN- WAITING – ME!	

MEN.
NO FANFARES

WOMEN.
OR SEDAN CHAIRS

MEN.
AND NO COACHES

WOMEN.
AND WE SOLD OUR BROACHES!

LEOPOLD.

NO AFTERNOON CARD GAMES WITH THE TSAR!

LILY.

NO CAVIAR!

BUT I SAY

WE'RE NOT DEAD NOW!

ARISTOCRATS.

WE'RE NOT DEAD NOW,

WE'RE IN FRANCE INSTEAD, NOW!

LILY. *(Takes command.)*

LET US NOT BE SAD!

THE NIGHT'S YOUNG,

AND RUSSIANS ARE MAD!

SO...

LET'S LIVE IN THE LAND OF YESTERDAY,

LIVE IN THE GRAND IMPERIAL HEYDAY.

LET'S LIVE IN THE LAND OF YESTERDAY RUSSIA!

ALL.

HUSHA!

LILY.	**ARISTOCRATS.**
LET'S PUT ON THE FANCY CLOTHES	OOH
AND LET'S WHILE OUR WOES AWAY	OOH

ALL.

IN RUSSIA,

LAND OF YESTERDAY.

LILY.

IN DIRE CIRCUMSTANCES,

WHY WALLOW IN REGRET?

WE'RE OUT OF SECOND CHANCES.

WHY ARE WE HERE, EXCEPT TO FORGET?

WE KNOW THE WORLD IS FICKLE.

LIFE IS A LEAKY SIEVE!

PASS ME A GLASS

AND GIVE ME A BOW –

AND DRINK TO THE "COUNTESS NOBODY" NOW!

WHY SHOULD I CARE
AS LONG AS I DARE TO LIVE?

ARISTOCRATS.

IN THE LAND OF YESTERDAY!

LILY.

LET'S RUN UP THE BILL
AS IF WE'RE STILL
ROYALTY AT PLAY

LILY & ARISTOCRATS.

IN RUSSIA, LAND OF YESTERDAY!

*(**LILY** and **THE OTHERS** dance.)*

*(By the end, **ALL** but the inexhaustible **LILY** fall to the floor. She continues to dance and drink until she notices they've collapsed. She rouses them in her own way.)*

LILY.

THE NIGHT'S YOUNG
AND RUSSIANS ARE MAD, SO...
LET'S LIVE IN THE LAND OF YESTERDAY.

ALL.

LIVE IN THE GRAND IMPERIAL HEYDAY.
LET'S LIVE IN THE LAND OF YESTERDAY RUSSIA!
HUSHA!

LILY.

LET'S BRUSH OFF THE DAYS OF OLD
AND LET'S HOLD THE WORLD AT BAY!

ALL.

YES, HERE'S TO

LILY.

RUSSIA!

ALL.

HERE'S TO RUSSIA!
HERE'S TO RUSSIA!
LAND OF YESTERDAY!

LILY.

OOH

ALL.

LAND OF YESTERDAY!

HEY!

> (**LILY** *ends up in* **VLAD**'*s arms. She's shocked to see him!*)

LILY. Vlad Popov! I thought the Bolsheviks put you in front of a firing squad.

VLAD. They did, but when they gave the order to fire, no one could pull the trigger.

LILY. I can't imagine why not.

VLAD. I still melt hearts, *ma chère,* just as you still melt mine.

[MUSIC NO. 19 "THE COUNTESS AND THE COMMON MAN"]

I crossed a continent for this moment.

> (*He devours her hand with kisses.*)

LILY. Still up to your old tricks!

VLAD. Admit you're happy to see me.

LILY. I'm glad you're not dead but that's as far as I'm prepared to go.

> (**LILY** *and* **VLAD** *move towards the garden. They will stroll during the following.*)

Scene Five
The Garden

LILY. What are you doing in Paris?

VLAD. Didn't you get my letter?

LILY. And I promptly tore it up.

VLAD. You've grown hard, my darling Lily.

LILY. No harder than I need be.

VLAD. My precious Lily.

LILY. I'm not the woman you remember, Vlad.

VLAD. No, you're even lovelier than I remember.

(He's already kissing her arm clear up to her shoulder.)

My hot-blooded, sensual, passionate mistress.

LILY. That was then: when the world was beautiful.

VLAD. We'll make it beautiful again – in Paris, the city for lovers.

LILY. If only we could.

VLAD. Ever since that first day I saw you at court, I knew I was beneath you.

LILY. You were right, darling, you were.

(She's falling in love with him again.)

VLAD.

I NOTICED YOU ACROSS A ROOM –
THE MOST EXQUISITE ROSE.
THE TINIEST TIARA AND
THAT HAUGHTY LITTLE NOSE.
I FLIRTED WITH YOU SHAMELESSLY

LILY.

OR SO THE SCANDAL GOES...
THE COUNTESS

VLAD.

AND THE COMMON MAN.
WE TIPTOED OFF TO PETERHOF
TO HAVE A ROYAL FLING.

LILY.

MY HUSBAND WAS OBLIVIOUS.
COUNTS NEVER KNOW A THING!

VLAD.

AND ALL OF IT WAS PERFECT...

LILY.

TILL YOU STOLE MY DIAMOND RING!

LILY & VLAD.

THE COUNTESS
AND THE COMMON MAN!

VLAD.

COLOGNE IN THE BEDCLOTHES,
THE PASTRY AND WINE,

LILY.

AND UNDER THE TABLE
YOUR FOOT TOUCHING MINE.

VLAD & LILY.

AND HOW MY HEART BEAT
WHEN YOU SENT ME "OUR SIGN"!

(They do "their sign.")

LILY.

I LOVED YOU...

VLAD.

YOU LOVED ME...
AND OH, IT WAS SIMPLY

VLAD & LILY.

DIVINE...

*(**VLAD** and **LILY** dance passionately until they're both dizzy and panting. They collect themselves and continue.)*

VLAD.

WHO WOULD HAVE KNOWN,
MY LITTLE ROSE,
WE'RE BACK WHERE WE BEGAN.

LILY.

AND I SUPPOSE

THAT YOU'LL PROPOSE
ANOTHER SNEAKY PLAN!
WHICH I'LL RESIST...

VLAD.
UNTIL YOU'RE KISSED...

(They kiss.)

VLAD & LILY.
FOR NOTHING'S BETTER THAN...

LILY.
THE COUNTESS

VLAD.
AND THE COMMON MAN...

VLAD & LILY.
THE COUNTESS AND THE COMMON MAN.

(They kiss. It's one for the ages!)

[MUSIC NO. 19A "REPRISE OF THE COUNTESS AND THE COMMON MAN AND LAND OF YESTERDAY"]

LILY. I'm waiting for you to kiss me again.

VLAD. Gladly, but first there's a young woman I want you to meet.

LILY. That's all?

VLAD. There'll be someone at the ballet on Monday who will want to meet her, too.

LILY. Who is that?

VLAD. The Dowager Empress. We're going to change history, Lily.

THE COUNTESS...

LILY.
AND THE COMMON MAN.

*(**VLAD** and **LILY** exit. **GLEB** appears from out of the shadows.)*

GLEB.
THEY LIVE IN THE LAND OF YESTERDAY,

LOST IN THEIR MAD IMPERIAL HEYDAY.
HOW SAD IS THEIR LAND OF YESTERDAY...
HOW COULD A GOOD RUSSIAN GIRL
BE SO BADLY LED ASTRAY?
YOU WANT TO CHANGE HISTORY?
WELL, I'LL LET YOU LEAD THE WAY...
TO ANYA...

Scene Six
Anya's Hotel Room

(**ANYA** *is sleeping fitfully.*)

[MUSIC NO. 20 "A NIGHTMARE"]

(*The* **THREE DAUGHTERS** *and* **YOUNG SON** *of the* **TSAR** *and* **TSARINA** *appear, almost like angels descending from Heaven in a pantomime.*)

OLGA, TATIANA & MARIA.
AH... AH... AH... AH...

ANYA. Who are you? Every night you come.

THE TSAR. And we will until you remember us.

OLGA, TATIANA & MARIA.
AH... AH... AH...

THE TSARINA.	**OLGA, TATIANA & MARIA.**
Have you said your prayers?	
God is everything.	AH...
Sleep well with this	AH...
mother's kiss.	AH...

OLGA, TATIANA & MARIA.
AH... AH...

(*The* **TSARINA** *kisses her much as she did in the Prologue. The* **TSAR** *looks sadly back at* **ANYA**. *They all do.*)

ALEXEI.	**OLGA, TATIANA & MARIA.**
Can I tell you a secret?	AH... AH...
I'm going to die soon.	AH...
We all are. Do you have a secret?	

ANYA. I don't know who I am.

ALEXEI. That's silly.

ALEXEI.	OLGA, TATIANA & MARIA.
Everyone knows who they are.	AH...

TSAR, TSARINA, & CHILDREN.
ANYA! ANYA! ANYA!

> *(The sound of a gunshot. **ANYA** wakes, terrified by her nightmare.)*

ANYA. Papa!

> *(**DMITRY** rushes in from the adjoining room.)*

DMITRY. Anya!

ANYA. The voices keep coming back!

DMITRY. That's all they are. Voices. You're having a nightmare.

ANYA. Stay with me, Dmitry, I'm frightened.

> *(He puts his arm around her.)*

DMITRY. Is that better?

ANYA. Who do you think I am, Dmitry?

DMITRY. If I were the Dowager Empress, I would want you to be Anastasia.

ANYA. You would?

DMITRY. I would want her to be a beautiful, strong, intelligent young woman.

ANYA. Is that what you think I am?

DMITRY. I do.

ANYA. Thank you.

DMITRY. You're welcome.

ANYA. I'd begun to wonder if you were ever going to pay me a compliment. Do you really think I might be her?

DMITRY. I want to believe you're the little girl I saw once many years ago.

[MUSIC NO. 21 "IN A CROWD OF THOUSANDS"]

ANYA. I don't understand.

DMITRY.

> IT WAS JUNE.
> I WAS TEN.
> I STILL THINK OF THAT DAY
> NOW AND THEN.
> A PARADE
> AND A GIRL,
> AND A CROWD OF THOUSANDS...
>
> SHE SAT STRAIGHT
> AS A QUEEN.
> ONLY EIGHT, BUT SO PROUD
> AND SERENE.
> HOW THEY CHEERED!
> HOW I STARED...
> IN THAT CROWD OF THOUSANDS!
>
> THEN I STARTED TO RUN
> AND TO CALL OUT HER NAME
> AS THE CROWD ON THE ROAD WENT WILD!
> I REACHED OUT WITH MY HAND,
> AND LOOKED UP...
> AND THEN
> SHE SMILED...
>
> THE PARADE
> TRAVELED ON.
> WITH THE SUN IN MY EYES,
> SHE WAS GONE.
> BUT IF I WERE STILL TEN
> IN THAT CROWD OF THOUSANDS
> I'D FIND HER
> AGAIN.

ANYA. You're making me feel I was there, too.

DMITRY. Maybe you were. Make it part of your story.

ANYA.

> A PARADE

DMITRY.

> A PARADE

ANYA.
>   PASSING BY.

DMITRY.
>   PASSING BY.

ANYA.
>   IT WAS HOT.
>   NOT A CLOUD IN THE SKY.
>   THEN A BOY CAUGHT MY EYE

ANYA & DMITRY.
>   IN A CROWD OF THOUSANDS.

ANYA.
>   HE WAS THIN.
>   NOT TOO CLEAN.
>   THERE WERE GUARDS,
>   BUT HE DODGED IN BETWEEN.
>   YES, HE MADE HIMSELF SEEN
>   IN THAT CROWD OF THOUSANDS!
>   THEN HE CALLED OUT MY NAME
>   AND HE STARTED TO RUN
>   THROUGH THE SUN AND THE HEAT AND CROWD.
>   AND I TRIED NOT TO SMILE,
>   BUT I SMILED...
>   AND THEN... HE BOWED!

DMITRY. I didn't tell you that.

ANYA. You didn't have to. I remember.

ANYA & DMITRY.
>   THE PARADE TRAVELED ON.
>   WITH THE SUN IN MY EYES,
>   YOU WERE GONE
>   BUT I KNEW EVEN THEN
>   IN A CROWD OF THOUSANDS
>   I'D FIND YOU
>   AGAIN.

>>   (**DMITRY** *bows to* **ANYA.** *It is the second time he has ever bowed to anyone.*)

DMITRY. Your highness.

Scene Seven
The Ballet

[MUSIC NO. 22 "ARRIVING AT THE BALLET / MEANT TO BE"]

(A movement sequence with underscore. The foyer of the theatre is a magnificent hall of marble steps and columns. It is bustling with pre-curtain activity. An attendant is ringing a handbell, urging everyone to their seats. Beautiful young women and men all dressed in the latest and highest fashion enter and present themselves for approbation.)

(Suddenly, a silence falls over the entranceway. **THE DOWAGER EMPRESS** *herself is in attendance. She is superbly gowned in black.* **LILY** *follows at a respectful distance.)*

*(***THE DOWAGER EMPRESS*** *moves on.* **LILY** *turns just in time to catch sight of* **VLAD** *in the crowd and gives him a smile or nod.)*

*(***VLAD*** *is wearing black tie and tails and has even managed to find a few old military decorations to pin to his jacket.)*

(As for **DMITRY,** *he looks elegant and handsome in his formal wear. He wears it with great aplomb, especially considering he's never been in such finery.* **VLAD** *tries to straighten* **DMITRY**'s *white tie and brush back an unruly lock of hair but* **DMITRY** *fidgets like a little boy)*

(A new sensation arrives in the lobby and there is a reaction to this new presence among them. It is **ANYA.** *She is transformed into the most beautiful young woman in Paris tonight.)*

*(**ANYA** has always liked the way **DMITRY** looks
but he has never looked like this. She takes
his arm, and he registers her beauty. **VLAD**
takes this in.)*

VLAD.
WHAT'S MEANT TO BE
IS MEANT TO BE.
I SEE IT AT A GLANCE.

SHE'S RADIANT
AND CONFIDENT
AND BORN TO TAKE THIS CHANCE.

I TRIED TO THINK
OF EVERYTHING.
I JUST FORGOT ROMANCE!

I NEVER SHOULD HAVE LET THEM DANCE.

*(The final warning bells are rung. **DMITRY**
and **ANYA** run to their places in the theatre,
looking for all the world like beautiful young
lovers.)*

*(**VLAD** stays behind a beat, watching them go.
He straightens his shoulders for the adventure
ahead.)*

Scene Eight
The Stage and Boxes

[MUSIC NO. 23 "QUARTET AT THE BALLET"]

(The curtain flies up and we are at the heart of Tchaikovsky's Swan Lake. *An elegant pas de deux holds center stage. You can hear a pin drop. People have stopped breathing. The* **DANCERS'** *discipline and technique are peerless.)*

(Slowly, the lights will shift to **ANYA, DMITRY,** *and* **VLAD** *in their box. Across the auditorium from them we will see* **THE DOWAGER EMPRESS** *and* **LILY** *in theirs.)*

(On the orchestra level or stalls, we see **GLEB.** *Everyone has a powerful pair of opera glasses;* **THE DOWAGER EMPRESS,** *a lorgnette.)*

*(*Swan Lake *continues among and between our protagonists. A very free use of space and perspective is asked for here. Imagine the dance.)*

*(***ANYA** *looks across the theatre to the box where* **THE DOWAGER EMPRESS** *can be seen. Is this her grandmother?* **THE DOWAGER EMPRESS** *looks across the theatre at this beautiful young woman staring at her through her opera glasses. Anastasia would be about the same age, she muses. But no, she is through playing these games with these pretenders.)*

(No one is more taken with **ANYA***'s transformation than* **GLEB** *as he watches her from afar.)*

ANYA.
CAN THIS BE THE EV'NING?

CAN THIS BE THE PLACE?
AM I ONLY DREAMING,
LOOKING AT HER FACE?
EVERYTHING I'VE WANTED
SUDDENLY SO CLEAR!
MY PAST AND MY FUTURE SO NEAR...

DMITRY.

NEXT TO ME THIS FRIGHTENED GIRL,
HOLDING TIGHT AS THE DANCERS WHIRL.
KEEP YOUR NERVE AND SEE THIS THROUGH.
IT'S WHAT YOU'VE COME TO DO...

THE DOWAGER EMPRESS.

SEE THAT GIRL.
COULD IT BE?
Don't be ridiculous!
I REFUSE TO DREAM.
I REFUSE TO HOPE.
I MUST STOP BELIEVING
I WILL EVER FIND HER...

GLEB.

SHE'S NEAR AT HAND,
YET HERE I STAND,
MY HEART AND MIND AT WAR...
THE TIMES MUST CHANGE
THE WORLD MUST CHANGE!
AND LOVE IS NOT WHAT REVOLUTION'S FOR...

DMITRY & GLEB.

SOMEONE HOLDS HER
SAFE AND WARM
SOMEONE RESCUES HER FROM THE STORM.
SIMPLE THINGS, BUT ONE THING'S CLEAR:
IT'S FATE THAT BROUGHT US HERE!

ANYA & THE DOWAGER EMPRESS.	**DMITRY.**	**GLEB.**
PAINTED WINGS,	HOME, LOVE,	SIMPLE THINGS.

ANYA & THE DOWAGER EMPRESS.	DMITRY.	GLEB.
SILVER SNOW,	FAM'LY.	SIMPLE THINGS!
WHIRLING LIKE A BALLET.	SHE WILL	AND WHATEVER I HAVE TO DO
	HAVE ALL OF IT!	I'LL DO.
THINGS MY HEART	I WILL	SIMPLE HOW
YEARNS TO KNOW.	HELP HER	SIMPLE MEN

ANYA, THE DOWAGER EMPRESS, DMITRY & GLEB.

FIND A WAY...

ANYA, THE DOWAGER EMPRESS, AUDIENCE.
DMITRY & GLEB.

ANASTASIA!	AH AH AH!

(The ballet ends. The **DANCERS** *step forward to receive their ovations and bouquets as we transition.)*

Scene Nine
The Anteroom of
the Dowager Empress' Box

(At the ballet. We can still hear the applause ringing in the auditorium proper.)

*(**LILY** opens the door leading from the box itself.)*

LILY. The finest and driest champagne they have, of course, Your Majesty.

*(She closes the door to the box as **VLAD** arrives.)*

VLAD. Is she in a good mood?

LILY. She's never in a good mood. What have you talked me into?

VLAD. Wait till you see her.

*(**ANYA** and **DMITRY** hurry into the anteroom.)*

*(**LILY** gasps at the sight of **ANYA** and spontaneously bows to her.)*

LILY. Your Highness.

ANYA. No, you mustn't.

*(She stops **LILY** from fully bowing.)*

VLAD. That composure! We did a good job, Dmitry.

LILY. I don't want to get your hopes up, young lady.

DMITRY. We'll celebrate after on your grandfather's bridge.

ANYA. *(Drawing herself up and to her full height.)* I'm ready.

DMITRY. *(Fully in charge of the situation now. It is his moment, too.)* You will announce the Grand Duchess Anastasia Nikolaevna Romanov.

*(**LILY** opens the door to the inner box itself.)*

LILY. You have a visitor, Your Majesty.

[MUSIC NO. 24 "EVERYTHING TO WIN"]

(ANYA goes through the door. LILY follows her. The door is closed behind them.)

DMITRY.

WHAT ARE THEY SAYING?
WONDER HOW LONG THEY'LL BE?
WHY SHOULD I WORRY?
WORRYING'S NOT LIKE ME!
NOTHING TO DO
BUT PACE AND STEW
AND WAIT TILL THE GIRL WALKS IN...
WHY PANIC NOW
WITH EV'RYTHING TO WIN...

VLAD.

My nerves can't take this. Tell Lily I needed a stiff glass of vodka.

(He hurries off, leaving DMITRY alone in the anteroom trying to hear what's going on. DMITRY paces, listens at the door.)

DMITRY.

NOTHING BUT SILENCE.
THIS COULD BE BAD,
BUT NO! LET'S ASSUME IT'S GOOD.
THOUGHT IT WAS FOOLPROOF.
NOTHING IS FOOLPROOF!
WHOA! BETTER KNOCK ON WOOD!
GIRL GETS A FAM'LY,
BOY GETS RICH!
AND FAIRYTALE GETS A SPIN!
HOW CAN WE FAIL
WITH EV'RYTHING TO WIN!

I WONDER
IF OUR PATHS
WILL EVER CROSS AGAIN...
THE WAY THEY DID
WHEN YOU WERE EIGHT

AND I WAS TEN...
WE SAID THIS WAS GOODBYE,
BUT EVEN SO
YOU NEVER KNOW...
YOU NEVER KNOW...

I SHOULD BE GLAD THAT
WE'RE BREAKING FREE, BUT
NOTHING IS WHAT IT WAS.
I DIDN'T KNOW
SHE MATTERED TO ME, BUT
NOW I CAN SEE SHE DOES...
CON MAN AND PRINCESS
GET THEIR WISH AND
FAIRYTALE COMES TRUE!
FUNNY, THE ONE SMALL PART
I NEVER KNEW...
WITH EV'RYTHING TO WIN
THE ONLY THING I LOSE
IS...

> *(**ANYA** enters through the door leading to the anteroom from the box seats. She is devastated.)*

What happened?

ANYA. She wouldn't even look at me. "Tell this impostor, Lily, I know her kind too well. She wants money and will break an old woman's heart to get it."

DMITRY. I'll tell her the truth.

ANYA. That I was a pawn in a scheme of yours? That you made me think I might be someone I never was or ever could be. I was cold and hungry and desperate when I met you, Dmitry, but I wasn't dishonest. I hate you for that.

> *(She goes. **DMITRY** hesitates whether to follow. **LILY** comes out.)*

LILY. I'm sorry, young man.

THE DOWAGER EMPRESS. *(Offstage.)* Is she gone?

(She enters. She stops at the sight of **DMITRY**.*)*

DMITRY. *(Despite himself.)* Your Royal Majesty.

THE DOWAGER EMPRESS. How dare you address me!

DMITRY. Anya doesn't want your money. I take full responsibility for bringing her to Paris.

THE DOWAGER EMPRESS. *Gendarmes!*

DMITRY. But I believe with all my heart that she is the Grand Duchess Anastasia.

THE DOWAGER EMPRESS. I will not stay for this.

> *(She turns to leave, but* **DMITRY** *boldly steps on the train of her gown and stops her.)*

DMITRY. She only wants what is rightfully hers: your recognition and your loving embrace. Try to imagine her life since her parents, sisters, little brother were murdered.

THE DOWAGER EMPRESS. I do not need reminding of what happened to my family. I lost everything I loved that day.

DMITRY. So did she. Anya survived for a reason: to heal what happened or Russia will be a wound that never heals.

> *(***THE DOWAGER EMPRESS** *slaps his face.)*

THE DOWAGER EMPRESS. That is no longer a concern of mine. Russia has damned itself to eternity for what it has done.

LILY. *(Concerned.)* You're tiring her.

DMITRY. God will judge you harshly, old woman. History already has.

> *(He goes.* **LILY** *starts to protest his turning his back on the* **THE DOWAGER EMPRESS** *but she waves this breech of etiquette away.)*

LILY. He turned his back to you!

THE DOWAGER EMPRESS. Take me home, Lily.

Scene Ten
The Hotel Rooms That Anya, Dmitry,
and Vlad Have Been Sharing

[MUSIC NO. 24A "TRANSITION TO HOTEL ROOM"]

(**ANYA** *is throwing things into a suitcase.
She is furious and heartbroken.* **DMITRY** *and*
VLAD *occasionally try to get a word in but
to little avail.* **ANYA** *is a perfect firestorm of
conflicting emotions. She is too angry to even
look at either of the two men.*)

ANYA. It was my life you played with. Telling me I was
someone else and letting me believe I was.

(*She picks up a little doll.*)

What is this?

DMITRY. I bought it for you when we were at that –

ANYA. I don't want it.

(*She throws it across the room.*)

DMITRY. Where are you going?

ANYA. Anywhere that's far from you.

VLAD. Anya!

ANYA. No wonder you were dismissed from court. Men
like you deserve every bad hand life deals you. You both
do.

[MUSIC NO. 24B "ANYA / HOTEL UNDERSCORE"]

(**LILY** *comes into the hotel room. She whispers
something to* **VLAD** *who whispers to* **DMITRY**.
The three of them will quickly step aside.)

(**THE DOWAGER EMPRESS** *enters.* **DMITRY** *and*
VLAD *bow their heads to her and quietly
withdraw with* **LILY**.)

(THE DOWAGER EMPRESS stands quietly as ANYA continues to hurl things into her suitcase.)

ANYA. I admired the way you were proud of who you were, despite your circumstances. You taught me to be the same – and the whole time you were tricking me.

(THE DOWAGER EMPRESS is clearly moved but remains silent. ANYA holds up a book.)

Russian history! Save it for your next Anastasia.

(She turns to throw the book at him but is astonished to see THE DOWAGER EMPRESS.)

Your Imperial Highness.

(She curtsies before THE DOWAGER EMPRESS.)

THE DOWAGER EMPRESS. I think history demands we play this game to the end.

ANYA. Please, be seated.

THE DOWAGER EMPRESS. There's no need. I shall be brief. Who are you?

ANYA. I believe I am the youngest daughter of –

THE DOWAGER EMPRESS. Spare me my family history! It's in every bookstore along the Seine. Anyone can read it.

ANYA. I didn't think you'd be so cruel.

THE DOWAGER EMPRESS. I'm old and impatient. Kindness has become a luxury.

ANYA. My Nana was the most loving woman imaginable.

THE DOWAGER EMPRESS. That was before they murdered everyone she loved.

ANYA. Her bosom smelled like oranges when she hugged me.

THE DOWAGER EMPRESS. It's a common enough scent.

ANYA. Not hers. It came from Sicily, made especially for her, in a box of polished olivewood.

(ANYA sits down.)

THE DOWAGER EMPRESS. How dare you sit without my permission!

(**ANYA** *leaps to her feet.*)

All right, sit. You have my permission.

(**ANYA** *sits.*)

In that case, I shall sit, too.

(*She sits.*)

Who was my favorite lady-in-waiting?

ANYA. You didn't have one. You kept dismissing them.

THE DOWAGER EMPRESS. It was a trick question. You're clever, I'll grant you that.

(*She studies* **ANYA** *carefully.*)

I'm trying to see the resemblance. I don't trust my eyes.

ANYA. You should wear spectacles.

(*At a harsh glare from her adversary.*)

I'm sorry.

THE DOWAGER EMPRESS. Name the three –

ANYA. Why don't you want me to be her?

THE DOWAGER EMPRESS. I have found solace in my bitterness. It doesn't disappoint me. You Anastasias always do.

ANYA. If you give me a chance, maybe I won't.

THE DOWAGER EMPRESS. I don't believe Anastasia exists.

ANYA. You don't want to believe it.

THE DOWAGER EMPRESS. What was your mother's full title as the Empress of All Russia?

ANYA. Aren't we beyond this?

THE DOWAGER EMPRESS. Her Imperial Majesty, the Empress of All the Russias, Alexandra Fyodorovna Roma –

ANYA. She was "Mama" to me. She was "Mama" to all of us.

(*She bursts into tears.*)

THE DOWAGER EMPRESS. You all cry at some point. Do you rehearse? Tears will get you nowhere.

ANYA. Why did you come here?

THE DOWAGER EMPRESS. Your young man told me you weren't part of his scheme.

ANYA. He's right, I wasn't.

THE DOWAGER EMPRESS. He believes that you very well may be my granddaughter. He says you've come to believe it yourself.

ANYA. I believe it with all my heart but I can't be her unless you recognize me.

THE DOWAGER EMPRESS. You can't be anyone unless you first recognize yourself.

ANYA. *(Bowing her head.)* I know.

THE DOWAGER EMPRESS. Do you know what it means to lose everything, young woman? My son, his children, everything I held dear and loved with all my heart – all lost and gone in one terrible moment.

> (**ANYA** *cowers at* **THE DOWAGER EMPRESS'** *force.*)

I'll ask you one last time, young woman, be very careful what you answer: who are you?

ANYA. I don't know anymore. Who are you?

THE DOWAGER EMPRESS. *(Sitting back a little at* **ANYA**'s *bluntness.)* An old woman who remembers everything the way it should have been and nothing the way it was.

ANYA. Do you remember the last time you saw Anastasia?

THE DOWAGER EMPRESS. *(Shaking her head.)* I didn't know it was the last time. We never do. We never know which goodbye is the last.

ANYA. You were leaving for Paris. You never came back. You gave her a music box. I believe this was it.

[MUSIC NO. 24C "ONCE UPON A DECEMBER (REPRISE)"]

(She opens the music box. It is out of tune and the mechanism is labored, but the music is potent. They listen to it together.)

FAR AWAY,
LONG AGO,
GLOWING DIM AS AN EMBER,

THE DOWAGER EMPRESS.
THINGS MY HEART USED TO KNOW...

THE DOWAGER EMPRESS & ANYA.
ONCE UPON A DECEMBER.

(*The tune continues.*)

ANYA. I said I'd come visit you in Paris. We'd go the ballet together and walk on Grandpapa's bridge.

THE DOWAGER EMPRESS. You never knew him. I loved him very much.

ANYA. We'll walk the bridge together for all of them, Nana.

THE DOWAGER EMPRESS. What took you so long?

ANYA. It doesn't matter, I'm here with you.

THE DOWAGER EMPRESS. Too late, you've come too late.

ANYA. It's never too late to come home, Nana.

THE DOWAGER EMPRESS. Anastasia.

(*She opens her arms to* **ANYA** *and embraces her.*)

ANYA. Orange blossoms.

Scene Eleven
A Private Reception Room
at a Luxurious Hotel

[MUSIC NO. 25 "THE PRESS CONFERENCE"]

(Preparations are underway for the introduction of **ANASTASIA** *to the world press and the Russian émigré society.* **LILY** *would seem to be in charge of the proceedings.* **VLAD** *is by her side.)*

(The following lines overlap chaotically and are not meant to be heard distinctly.)

FRENCH. A question from the French press...

RUSSIAN. On behalf of all Russian Expatriots, may I ask...

GERMAN. Germany demands equal time!

FRENCH. We want the truth!

RUSSIAN. Your attention, please!

GERMAN. We have the right to know!

FRENCH. Excuse me, over here!

REPORTERS GROUP #1.

HAS SHE BEEN LIVING FAR OR NEAR?

REPORTERS GROUP #2.

WHAT KIND OF LETTER DID SHE SEND?

SOLO REPORTER. *(Spoken in rhythm.)*

EXCUSE ME, OVER HERE!

ALL.

THE RUMORS NEVER END.

REPORTERS GROUP #1.

YOU'VE HAD IMPOSTERS, IS IT TRUE?

REPORTERS GROUP #2.

WHAT SORT OF PROOF DO YOU INTEND?

SOLO REPORTER. *(Spoken in rhythm.)*

EXCUSE ME, OVER HERE!

REPORTERS.

THE RUMORS NEVER END!

*(**REPORTER** hubbub.)*

LILY. *(Shuts them up.)* Good afternoon. I am the Countess Malevsky-Malevitch. And this is *Count* Vladimir Popov.

VLAD. *(Spoken in rhythm.)*
P-O-P-O-V!

LILY.
THE DOWAGER IS COMING
BUT SHE'S RUNNING VERY LATE.
I'M CERTAIN THAT HER MAJESTY
WILL SET THE RECORD STRAIGHT.
BUT ROYALTY IS ROYALTY.
ONE ALWAYS TO WAIT –

(More clamor.)

I'M REALLY NOT AT LIBERTY
TO GOSSIP WITH THE PRESS!
HER MAJESTY IS COMING
AND TILL THEN YOU'LL HAVE TO GUESS!

VLAD. *(Spills the beans.)*
SUFFICE TO SAY YOU'LL MEET TODAY
THE LITTLE LOST PRINCESS!

*(**LILY** is ready to kill him. The **REPORTERS** go wild.)*

MALE REPORTERS #1 & #5.
DID SHE ARRIVE BY TRAIN?

MALE REPORTER #2.
I HEARD SHE MAY HAVE GONE INSANE!

LILY. *(Spoken in rhythm.)*
A LIE!

MALE REPORTER #3.
I'M FROM THE *PARIS NEWS*.
WE DO EXCLUSIVE INTERVIEWS.

VLAD. *(Pleased at the thought of PR. Spoken in rhythm.)*
OH MY!

MALE REPORTER #4.
IS SHE A FAKE OR IS SHE REAL?

FEMALE REPORTER #1. *(Spoken in rhythm.)*
> HOW DOES SHE LOOK?

FEMALE REPORTER #2.
> HOW DOES SHE FEEL?

FEMALE REPORTERS #3 & #4.
> WHAT HAS SHE DONE? WHERE HAS SHE BEEN?

FEMALE REPORTERS.
> HOW DID SHE LIVE? WHO TOOK HER IN?

LILY.
> WE'RE NEARLY READY TO BEGIN!

REPORTERS GROUP #1.	**REPORTERS GROUP #2.**	**2 SOPRANOS.**
WHERE HAS SHE BEEN? WHAT HAS SHE DONE?		THE RUMOR!
	WHO TOOK HER IN? IS SHE THE ONE?	THE LEGEND!
WE'RE WAITING EAGERLY TO SEE		THE MYSTERY!
IS SHE	IS SHE	

ALL.
> THE PRINCESS ANASTASIA!

2 SOPRANOS..
> ANASTASIA!

> (**LILY** *whistles to get their attention.*)

LILY.
> NOW...
> HER MAJESTY IS ELDERLY
> AND DOESN'T SUFFER
> FOOLS.

REPORTERS.
> SHE DOESN'T

LILY.	REPORTERS.
SHE'S READY TO RECEIVE YOU	SUFFER FOOLS!
BUT YOU MUST OBEY THE RULES.	WE MUST OBEY
NO SMOKING	THE RULES!
AND NO JOKING!	

VLAD.

AND NO HANDLING THE JEWELS.

LILY. *(Spoken in rhythm.)*

MEMBERS OF THE PRESS,

(Sung.)

THIS WAY!

REPORTERS.	2 SOPRANOS.
WHERE HAS SHE BEEN?	THE RUMOR!
WHAT HAS SHE DONE?	
WHO TOOK HER IN?	THE LEGEND!
IS SHE THE ONE?	
WE'RE WAITING EAGERLY TO SEE	THE MYSTERY!
THE PRINCESS	

REPORTERS & SOPRANOS.

ANASTASIA!

> **(LILY** *sweeps* **VLAD** *away, followed by*
> **REPORTERS.***)*

Scene Twelve
An Anteroom

(THE DOWAGER EMPRESS enters with ANYA, and they have their picture taken. ANYA is wearing a bejeweled royal gown and a tiara for her presentation to the world's press.)

THE DOWAGER EMPRESS. Press and fellow Russians, they're all going to want to take a look at you and ask some questions.

LEOPOLD. Surely, Your Majesty, you don't think this...this *impostor* is the Grand Duchess Anastasia.

ANYA. *(Clearly recognizing him.)* Count Leopold, with your dyed-hair, powdered-face, and vodka breath, no wonder my parents laughed at you behind your back.

THE DOWAGER EMPRESS. *(Delighted.)* You're right, Anastasia, they did!

VLAD. *(Emboldened.)* Everyone did, Your Majesty.

THE DOWAGER EMPRESS. *(Scowling.)* I remember you.

LILY. *(Low.)* Quit while you're ahead, Vlad.

VLAD. Yes, Your Majesty. Thank you, Your Majesty. Goodbye, Your Majesty.

> *(He quickly exits backwards, bowing all the way.)*

THE DOWAGER EMPRESS. I don't like that man.

LILY. He's not so bad.

> *(At a look from THE DOWAGER EMPRESS.)*

Yes, he is, Your Majesty, he's a terrible person.

> *(LILY exits hastily.)*

THE DOWAGER EMPRESS. Get used to people agreeing with everything you say.

ANYA. That's not right.

THE DOWAGER EMPRESS. Now where's your young man?

ANYA. He's not my young man.

THE DOWAGER EMPRESS. If it's not plain to you that he loves you – !

ANYA. He's not my young man, Nana!

THE DOWAGER EMPRESS. When he refused my reward for finding you, I thought, "Anastasia has found herself another kind of prince – one of character, not birth."

ANYA. Dmitry refused the reward?

THE DOWAGER EMPRESS. You are Anastasia. He said that was his reward. You have made this the happiest day of my life, Anastasia. Make sure it will be yours as well, Anya.

[MUSIC NO. 25A "EVERYTHING TO WIN (REPRISE)"]

We will always have each other, no matter what you decide.

> *(She goes.* **ANYA** *ponders her situation: will she give up Dmitry to be with her grandmother?)*

ANYA.

I SHOULD BE GLAD
I'M WHERE I SHOULD BE,
BUT NOTHING IS WHAT IT WAS.
I DIDN'T KNOW
HE MATTERED TO ME,
BUT NOW I CAN SEE HE DOES...
CON MAN AND PRINCESS
GET THEIR WISH AND
FAIRYTALE COMES TRUE!
THE ONLY THING I LOSE
IS...

> *(She has made her mind up. She will find Dmitry before he goes. As she turns to go she is confronted by* **GLEB**.*)*

Gleb!

GLEB.

AN UNDERHANDED GIRL
AN ACT OF DESPERATION
AND TO MY CONSTERNATION

I LET YOU GO...

...but not this time. Paris is no place for a good and loyal Russian.

ANYA. We are both good and loyal Russians.

GLEB. I've come to take you home.

ANYA. My home is here now.

GLEB. Stop playing this game, Anya, I beg you.

ANYA. We both know it's not a game, Gleb.

GLEB. If you are Anastasia, do you think history wants you to have lived?

ANYA. Yes! Why don't you?

[MUSIC NO. 26 "STILL / THE NEVA FLOWS (REPRISE)"]

GLEB. The Romanovs were given everything and they gave back nothing – until the Russian people rose up and destroyed them.

ANYA. All but one. Finish it. I am my father's daughter.

GLEB. I am my father's son. Finish it I must.

(The **ROMANOVS** *appear, backing away from the* **SOLDIERS.** **GLEB** *is engulfed by these terrifying memories.)*

ROMANOVS & SOLDIERS.

AH... AH...

GLEB.

MY FATHER SHOOK HIS HEAD
AND TOLD ME NOT TO ASK.
MY MOTHER SAID HE DIED OF SHAME.

ANYA.   **MEN & WOMEN.**

In me, you see them.   AH AH
Look at their faces in
mine, hear their screams,   AH AH AH
imagine their terror.

GLEB.

BUT I BELIEVE HE DID
A PROUD AND VITAL TASK

GLEB.	MEN & WOMEN.
AND IN MY FATHER'S NAME...	AH AH

ANYA.

Do it. Do it and I will be   AH AH AH AH
with my parents and my
brother and sisters all
over again.

*(**GLEB** takes out a revolver.)*

GLEB.

THE CHILDREN! THEIR VOICES!
A MAN MAKES PAINFUL CHOICES!
HE DOES WHAT'S NECESSARY,
ANYA!

FOR RUSSIA, MY BEAUTY,
WHAT CHOICE BUT SIMPLE DUTY?
WE HAVE THE PAST TO BURY,
ANYA...

VOICES.

AND THE NEVA FLOWS,
A NEW WIND BLOWS,

GLEB & VOICES.

AND SOON IT WILL BE SPRING.
THE LEAVES UNFOLD.
THE TSAR LIES COLD!

GLEB. For the last time. Who are you?

ANYA. I am the Grand Duchess Anastasia Nikolaevna Romanov.

*(**GLEB** raises the pistol and cocks it.)*

GLEB.

BE CAREFUL WHAT A DREAM MAY BRING...
A REVOLUTION IS A SIMPLE...

(The pause is interminable.)

I can't!

(He lets the gun fall and sobs.)

ANYA. I mean you no harm, Gleb.

(She puts her hand on his head in a gesture of forgiveness.)

GLEB. I believe you are Anastasia.

ANYA. What will you tell them?

GLEB. That I was not my father's son, after all. Long life, comrade.

*(**GLEB** and **ANYA** shake hands. He goes.)*

Scene Thirteen
The Grand Ballroom
at the Luxurious Hotel

[MUSIC NO. 27 "FINALE"]

(The press conference is about to begin. **THE DOWAGER EMPRESS** *has never looked more regal or beautiful.)*

*(***LILY*** *is anxious.* **THE DOWAGER EMPRESS** *is strangely serene.)*

LILY. She'll turn up but why would she disappear in the first place? You've accepted her as the heir to the Romanov fortune. She'll live like a queen, even though people don't want queens anymore. Well, the English do but they're crazy.

*(***VLAD*** *returns. He carries the music box.)*

VLAD. Not a trace of her. The room was bare except for this.

*(***THE DOWAGER EMPRESS*** *takes the music box from him. She knows now.)*

THE DOWAGER EMPRESS. I think we have seen the last of that young woman, Lily.

LILY. Was she Anastasia?

*(***THE DOWAGER EMPRESS***, *remembering:)*

THE DOWAGER EMPRESS. You're my favorite. Strong, not afraid of anything.

VLAD. It's time, Your Imperial Majesty. They can't hold them any longer.

Scene Fourteen
The Alexander Bridge

(**ANYA** *runs on. There is no trace of* **DMITRY**. *What has she done for love?*)

(**DMITRY** *enters. He has his old battered suitcase and has changed back into his old clothes. He looks very much like he did when we first met him.*)

DMITRY. If you ever see me from a carriage again, don't wave, don't smile. I don't want to be in love with someone I can't have for the rest of my life. Goodbye, Your Majesty.

ANYA. I always dreamed my first kiss would be in Paris with a handsome prince.

DMITRY. I'm not your prince, Anya.

ANYA. The Grand Duchess Anastasia would beg to disagree...

(*She's wanted to call him this for a long time.*)

...Dima.

(*She kisses him. It is mutual.*)

(*They embrace and exit together. Music continues throughout the rest.*)

Scene Fifteen
The Hotel Ballroom /
a Government Office

(THE DOWAGER EMPRESS enters the press conference.)

(THE REPORTERS quiet down.)

THE DOWAGER EMPRESS. As of today, there will be no more Anastasias.

(Consternation. She waits for it to end.)

The reward for her safe return will be given to charity.

(Applause for this statement. Lights up on **GLEB** *back in his full Chekist uniform. He "bookends"* **THE DOWAGER EMPRESS.***)*

GLEB. *(Straight front, as if delivering a report.)* There never was an Anastasia. She was a dream.

THE DOWAGER EMPRESS. A beautiful dream.

GLEB. A dream that only time will fade.

THE DOWAGER EMPRESS. So, no more talk of the Grand Duchess Anastasia Romanov.

GLEB. The new order has no need for fairytales. The case is closed.

THE DOWAGER EMPRESS. Still...

ALL.
FAR AWAY
LONG AGO

ALL OTHERS.	**ENSEMBLE WOMEN.**
GLOWING DIM AS AN EMBER	AH AH

ALL.
THINGS MY HEART USED TO KNOW...
ONCE UPON A DECEMBER

*(***ANYA** *and* **DMITRY** *are surrounded by the*

members of the Romanov family. **ANYA** *sees her younger self as in the Prologue. The past and the present have been reunited.* **ANYA** *and her prince can dance all the way back to St. Petersburg. They are the stuff of dreams. They belong to all of us.)*

End of Act II

[MUSIC NO. 28 "BOWS"]

[MUSIC NO. 29 "EXIT MUSIC"]